GIRLS' LIFE MAGAZINE

GL The Girls' Life Big Book of Short Stories

Edited by
Karen Bokram

Illustrated by
Frank Montagna

Scholastic Inc.

New York • Toronto • London • Auckland • Sydney
Mexico City • New Delhi • Hong Kong • Buenos Aires

ISBN 0-439-44981-2

Design: Mark Neston
Illustrations: Frank Montagna/www.artscounselinc.com

12 11 10 9 8 7 6 5   5 6 7 8/0

Printed in the U.S.A.

First Scholastic printing, July 2003

Contents

Get Reading!

Short stories are great! You know why? 'Cause they're, well, short. You can easily read them in one sitting, and just about anywhere— sitting under a tree during lunch, in bed for ten minutes just before you fall asleep, waiting at the doctor's office, wherever...whenever. You never have to wonder what's going to happen in the next chapter because short stories cut right to the chase. You still get to use your imagination—but with immediate gratification! Not a bad deal.

And while short stories are fictional, some of 'em seem so real that you can practically picture yourself as one of the characters. Especially when they're about girls like you! And, hey, you can start reading at the end of the book if you want, skip to the front, and finish up in the middle—you know, shake things up a bit.

At *GL,* we love short stories. So much that we actually have a special contest every year to give girls a chance to share their own short stories. You'll find two such stories in this collection (*The Anonymous Birthday Club* and *The Crush Crisis*). Want to become a famous fiction writer? Log on to www.girlslife.com, and go to the *You Wrote It* section. You never know—we might feature your short story in our next anthology!

Karen

Karen Bokram
Editor-in-Chief, *GL*

Popularity Rules

Kristi Collier Thompson

*If you want to fit in with the popular crowd,
you have to play by the rules.*

I glanced around carefully to make sure no one was looking. Then, I pulled out my little blue notebook and made an entry. **Rule #22:** *Never beat Amelia Tanner at anything—especially when others are watching.*

Amelia had been going on and on all week about the free-skate competition. She even had a new ballerina-pink costume for the big event. And for Stephanie to win…well, as excited as I was for my BFF, I couldn't help but notice the look of contempt on Amelia's face. To make matters worse, Josh Harrington, the hunky hockey forward, high-fived Stephanie in front of the entire school, practically. That move broke **Rule #4:** *Never flirt with a guy who used to go out with someone more popular than you.* And particularly not Amelia Tanner's ex-boyfriend.

Stephanie didn't even seem to notice her flagrant violation of the Rules. I jotted myself a note to talk to her about it just as soon as I got the chance.

Amelia called me the next day. "You will never believe what Stephanie just said to me," she barked. "She was all, 'I can't believe I won! Can you believe I won? I won! I won! That was so amazing! I won.'" Amelia pitched her voice high and sing-song. I sprawled across my bed, letting my head hang over the edge so all the blood rushed to my face.

"She did not," I replied, already trying not to take sides.

"She so *did*. She was totally bragging, Jen," Amelia retorted.

I sat up quickly. Ow. Head rush. I blinked rapidly as my room did a slow-motion spin.

"Really? She was bragging?"

I glanced at my little blue notebook and the note to call Stephanie. Bragging broke **Rule #7:** *No matter how good you are, never, ever brag about how good you are in front of someone popular, unless she brags about you first.*

"Totally. She's on this huge ego trip," added Amelia.

I hung up the phone. *No way!* I told myself. *No way Stephanie would act that way.* I knew my best friend better than anyone. But I remembered **Rule #8**: *It doesn't matter what you say and do. It only matters what other people* think *you say and do.*

Katie called next. "Stephanie is so on my nerves," she said.

"She is?" I felt a knot of apprehension settle into the pit of my stomach. I twisted my hair 'round and 'round my finger until it stuck in a tangled mass next to my scalp. "Ouch!"

"What?"

"Nothing." I held the cordless phone against my ear with my shoulder and worked with the other hand to free my finger. "What did she do?"

"Lisa Thornton, the brainiac, asked her if they could be partners for the science fair, and Stephanie said 'yes.'"

"So?"

"So...now I'm stuck with Harvey Gerber as *my* partner."

I cringed. Harvey Gerber still picked his nose when he thought no one was looking. That broke **Rule #2**: *Never leave a popular classmate stranded with a social reject for group projects.*

This was getting serious. I needed to talk to Stephanie right away and do some major damage control.

It had taken Stephanie and me a solid year to move from shy, nerdy mode to second-most-popular status—right where we'd always wanted to be. We weren't quite as cool as Amelia and Katie, so we couldn't step on their toes or we'd be knocked down the popularity pole. Most popular was too much trouble. Those girls were either super-rich or ultra-beautiful. They also seemed mega-dumb. And nobody liked them much, which made it hard to understand why they were popular in the first place. No, they weren't worth the effort. But second-most-popular, like Amelia and Katie? Perfect! Of course, there were these Rules....

"I'm tired of the Rules," Stephanie said when I called her. "I want to have fun. I like Josh Harrington, and I think he likes me." She giggled. "Isn't he *sooo* cute? And Lisa Thornton is planning this really great science project with baby ducklings. All Katie wants to do is cut out pictures from magazines and paste them to poster board. Besides, Harvey Gerber isn't *that* bad."

"But, Stephanie!" I begged and pleaded and tried to explain. We had worked so hard to become second-most-populars. First, we had to go undercover and actually discover the Rules—it's not like they were written down somewhere. At least, not until I compiled them in my little blue notebook. And *that* wasn't easy. We shadowed the second-most-popular girls everywhere—like spies. It took us months to crack their code. One thing we learned for sure during our year-in-training—break the Rules and you are in extreme danger of careening down the popularity scale faster than that ride at the amusement park that drops you like a falling elevator.

"Don't worry about it, Jen," Stephanie assured me, as I searched my closet for something to wear to school the next day. I was glad my birthday was coming up soon. I needed some new clothes. **Rule #15:** *Popular people are only allowed to wear the latest and coolest clothes.* Then she added, "It's no big deal. Amelia and Katie will forget all about it."

I held up a pair of hip-huggers and studied my reflection in the mirror. "I hope so," I said.

◆ ◆ ◆

They didn't forget. And I learned a new Rule: It's not difficult to become totally ostracized from the school social scene. No one made an announcement that Stephanie was now an outcast. It just sort of happened. It was like she had caught this awful disease or something and no one wanted to be around her. By Tuesday morning, Stephanie Williams, former member of the second-most-populars, was a social outcast. And I was trying hard to figure out how to keep myself from getting ousted, too. I stopped answering my phone. I couldn't bear to tell Stephanie I wouldn't be able to talk to her anymore. **Rule #5**: *Don't associate with social outcasts.*

It took Stephanie a few days to catch on. I mean, no one wanted to come right out and tell her she was yesterday's news. She still ate lunch at the second-most-popular girls' table, right next to me and across from Amelia. But no one would talk to her, at least not directly.

"Hi, Jen," Stephanie said on Wednesday. She put her tray on the table, and then slid into the seat. "What's up?"

I swallowed and glanced at Amelia. **Rule #3**: *When in doubt about how to act, always copy the actions of someone who is more popular than you are.* Amelia rolled her eyes heavenward. I did the same. While I was looking that way, I offered up a little prayer, hoping something, *anything*, might get Stephanie back into the good graces of the group.

Stephanie looked from me to Amelia and back again. "Why are you guys acting like such jerks?" she asked.

So much for divine intervention, I thought with a groan. **Rule #11**: *Never criticize someone popular in a voice loud enough for anyone to hear.*

"Fine!" Stephanie declared. She turned her back to us and jabbed her food with a fork. My heart clutched. This was awful. I stared at Amelia, pleading with her to break the silence, but she kicked me under the table.

"Ow," I groaned. I reached down and rubbed my shin.

"What's wrong?" Stephanie asked. Her face wore a look of concern. I wanted to crawl under the table and blend in with the tile floor. But there was probably a Rule against that, too.

"Hey, Katie," Amelia said before I could answer. "Jen and I keep hearing this strange voice but, when we look, no one is there."

Katie laughed, and so did Amelia. I concentrated on expertly dunking my Tater Tots into a big glob of ketchup. I didn't want to see Stephanie's face.

I knew Stephanie hated what was happening. I watched her between classes. Once, I caught her crying, and another time, I saw her sneak into the school counselor's office. That broke **Rule #14:** *Never rag on a popular person to a faculty member.* I had to do something quick! On Friday, after lunch period, I waited until no one else was around, and I grabbed Stephanie and dragged her into the girls' bathroom.

"You have to apologize," I whispered fiercely behind the bolted door of the restroom stall. "Here," I handed her the little blue notebook. "**Rule #21** talks about how to get back into the good graces of the group." Stephanie shook her head sadly. She gave me back the notebook. "I *can't*," she said.

"Yes, you can." I flipped to the page with **Rule #21** to show her. "See. It's not that hard."

"What I mean is, I don't *want* to."

"You don't *want* to? But...I don't understand. I thought you were my best friend." I felt tears welling up behind my eyes. And I felt a little sick.

"And, I thought *you* were *my* best friend," Stephanie said. "At least, I still want you to be. But the other girls, well, I don't like them all that much anymore. I'm having lots more fun with Lisa and Josh and...."

"Stephanie!" I snapped the notebook shut and looked around to see if anyone was eavesdropping. "Don't say that!"

Stephanie shrugged. "I'm sorry, Jen."

The next week, Stephanie moved from our lunch table to sit with Lisa Thornton's group—a group so far off the popularity chart that they didn't even count. That broke **Rule #6:** *Stay as close as possible to popular people at all times.* And it definitely showed a blatant disrespect for **Rule #12:** *Never get caught eating lunch with the unpopular.*

"Well, I guess we know where Stephanie belongs," Amelia said in her snootiest voice. I glared at her and thought about telling her where *she* could go sit, but then I clamped my mouth shut. I couldn't. I just couldn't. I clutched my little blue notebook tightly in my hands. I had worked too hard to be accepted by the second-most-populars.

◆ ◆ ◆

My birthday was two weeks later, on February 14. Kind of corny, sharing a birthday with Valentine's Day, but at least it didn't break any Rules. And it meant I always got a Valentine from someone. During lunch, the second-most-populars gave me a gigantic peanut-butter heart. It was really pretty. I guess they just forgot that I'm allergic to peanuts.

I tried to have fun. All the other girls were laughing and eating and having a great time, which adhered to **Rule #1**: *Always act in a way that makes other, less popular people wish they were you.*

Halfway through lunch, Stephanie walked by our table, pushed a small, gift-wrapped box in front of me, and then quickly walked away.

I sat stunned for a moment and glanced around. No one else seemed to have noticed. I opened the card: *"Happy birthday, Jen! You don't have to say thanks or anything. I understand the Rules. I just want you to have this. BFF, Stephanie."*

My mouth felt like cotton as I slowly unwrapped the present. I opened the box and pulled out a black-beaded bracelet with red interlocking hearts. It was beautiful. I knew Stephanie had made it. She had gotten a jewelry-making kit for Christmas.

"What is *that*?" Amelia asked. She snorted and brought me back to reality. **Rule #19**: *Homemade gifts are way uncool, except the ones from maybe your grandma.*

"It's a present," I said. I licked my lips. "From Stephanie." I clipped the bracelet around my wrist and held it up.

"From Stephanie? Eww." Katie wrinkled up her nose.

I looked at Amelia and Katie and the other second-most-populars. They rolled their eyes and grimaced. Then, they went back to eating, laughing, and gossiping. I watched them for a few minutes. Everything seemed to start moving at a snail's pace.

That's when I stood up and walked across the cafeteria, winding my way past tables and chairs. I saw Stephanie loading her empty lunch tray on the conveyor belt.

"Hey, Steph," I called. "Thank you. For the bracelet." I held up my arm and showed her.

Stephanie shrugged. "You're welcome, Jen. Happy birthday." She turned to walk away.

"Hey, wait," I said. "I'm…uh…I'm having a party for my birthday. Do you want to come?"

She paused. "I'm not sure. Who else will be there?"

An alarm went off in my brain. **Rule #10:** *If you throw a party, everyone in the group must be invited.*

I stopped and looked back toward the second-most-populars. They were still eating and laughing. No one seemed to notice that I had left the table. I wondered if they would *ever* notice.

"No one else," I declared. "Just you!"

Stephanie grinned. She grabbed my arm and walked me toward the table where Lisa Thornton, Josh Harrington, and her other new friends were sitting. Along the way, I stopped and dumped my little blue notebook in the trash can. Amidst banana peels and sandwich wrappers, I could still read the words on the cover—POPULARITY RULES.

Being the Bigger Person

Emilie Ostrander

*Minnie is positive she got the short end of the stick.
Then came along a **big** idea...*

"Arms up," the seamstress at the costume store said as she pinched handfuls of fabric between her fingers, sliding pins through the folds. "Four inches on each side." She shook her head as she wrote down the measurements. "Wow," she murmured. "You sure are tiny!"

"Fabulous observation," I wanted to say. "You can sew *and* notice the obvious. Very impressive!"

The seamstress hiked the green fabric above my knees. "Is this where you want it, dear?" she asked.

I looked in the mirror. "Uhmm-hmm," I nodded. "That's good."

She made some marks on her order form. "Okay, we'll take off six inches," she said, as her hand moved in loopy strokes. "So, just how tall are you?"

I sighed. "Four-foot-ten," I said, mechanically. I knew the drill.

She wrinkled up her nose. "And how *old* are you?"

"Almost 14," I braced myself and looked at my best friend, Lindy, in the mirror. She was sitting on the dressing room bench, toying with her ponytail. She looked up and gave me the look that said, "Here we go again."

"Wow," the seamstress said, again. I knew what was coming next. "I would have thought you were only 11."

The little-kid comment was getting so old. No one needed to tell me I was short. I already knew.

"So, you're going as Tinkerbell to a costume party?" the seamstress asked, pulling at the slumping, way-too-big left wing.

"No," I clarified, reaching over my shoulder to perk up my wing. "It's a costume dance, our May Mixer."

"Like a masquerade ball?"

I nodded. She was sort of right, except our school "ball" is held in the North Gym, decorated with paper streamers.

She eyed the little yellow fairy slippers I had bought for the occasion and gave out a laugh, "Honey, you can save your money because you practically *are* Tinkerbell!"

Lindy cleared her throat and said, "Minnie doesn't have blonde hair like Tinkerbell. Besides, Minnie's got at least three good inches on Tinkerbell." The seamstress laughed at Lindy's joke and left the dressing room.

I should've been used to it. I mean, for the last 13 (almost 14!) years of my life, I've been way shorter than everyone. I kind of stretched the truth when I said I was four-foot-ten. I'm actually four-foot-nine and three-quarters.

So, what's it like being the smallest kid in school? For starters, the kids I baby-sit every Wednesday are practically taller than I am — and they're third-graders.

Adults always tell me I don't look like I attend junior high school. I try to laugh it off. I'm even enough of a sport to let people call me Minnie instead of Melinda. That said, it just doesn't seem funny anymore. Seems I'm everyone's favorite short joke.

"You really *do* look cute," Lindy said, folding her own costume into a neat square. She was going as a genie. Lindy is tall and even has curves. Her costume didn't need a stitch of alterations.

"Cute? Tell that to Jeff Jackson."

Lindy rolled her eyes. "He doesn't know what he's missing." She stood up and unlocked the dressing room door.

I had asked Jeff to the May Mixer, but he said he just wanted to "be friends," which is probably code for he thinks I'm a little kid, too.

It was humiliating to get shot down. Especially since Lindy and Claudia had dates. I told the girls I'd just stay home.

"But the theme is 'Queen of Hearts and Other Magical Girls'," Lindy had protested. "You *have* to go. You've always said you're looking for a good excuse to be Tinkerbell."

"No, I didn't. When did I ever say that?"

"Okay, you didn't—I made it up. But will you go anyhow?" Lindy shot back.

"Why not?" I figured. But I still felt hopeless about guys. *I am not your kid sister! Look at me differently!* But, that's the problem—guys *do* notice I'm different.

It was fun at first. I even liked the attention. It was cool knowing all our guy friends think I'm cute because I'm little. But, now, I'd prefer that the guys think of me as pretty, not cute.

I told that to Lindy after we left the costume store and found a table at the food court. "Louis Tidmore likes you for you," she said before slurping her soda.

"That's my consolation prize?" I asked, rolling up my straw wrapper and flicking it at her. "*Louis Tidmore?*"

She smiled. "That's right, Buttercup!"

Since second grade, I've been the only girl shorter than Louis. Hence, it made me his automatic love interest. In fifth grade, he cut off one of my brown curls to keep in his desk. In sixth grade P.E., we were paired as square-dancing partners, and it was the happiest gym class of his life!

And last semester in health class, Louis made sure we were paired together for a project in which we had to pretend we were married and organize a household budget. I was absent the day we picked partners and unable to defend myself.

I reminded Lindy of Louis' and my failed marriage. "My favorite was when he wrote 'Dr. Louis and Mrs. Minnie Tidmore' on all the assignments he turned in," she recalled gleefully.

"That's not funny," I said.

◆ ◆ ◆

Lindy checked the drama bulletin board the next morning to see if we'd been cast as dancers. The list was posted high, and kids were crowded in front of it, blocking my view, so I hung back.

I saw Lindy run her finger down the list of names twice, like she was looking for something that wasn't there. She squeezed her way out of the crowd. "Well?" I asked. "Did we get it?"

Lindy hugged her blue binder to her chest. "Not exactly," she said, slowly. "I got dancer, but you sort of didn't." She shifted her voice to a happier tone. "But you did get a speaking part in the play!"

"Really? Which part?" I asked.

Lindy's eyes darted around the room as she shifted from one foot to the next.

"Okay, great. What am I?" I asked.

Lindy took a deep breath and broke the news. "You're the telegram boy." I pictured myself as a telegram boy: short wig, button-down shirt, pair of knickers. No way! Very uncool to make the short girl a boy.

I told my older brother, Stan, about my part in the play, when I met him by his car for a ride home that afternoon. I was hitting him up for some sympathy, which I definitely did not get.

"No big deal," Stan said, unlocking the passenger door so his best friend, Will, could climb in the front seat.

"Go ahead," Will motioned for me to hop in. "I can take the back seat." Will always offers me the front seat. He's so considerate. I have no clue how he tolerates dorky, no-manners Stan.

"I can sit in back. After you," I said.

"Ladies first," he insisted, and I could feel myself blushing.

Stan leaned over from the driver's seat and peered out the passenger-side door. "Ladies first?" he joked, looking around the parking lot. "I don't see a lady—just Will and a telegram boy."

"Whatever," I shot back.

Will rolled his eyes in response. "Hey, it's a speaking role, Min." And to my brother he added, "Leave her alone, Stan."

◆ ◆ ◆

The next day, I was hoping a little talk with Mrs. Sharpp, the musical director, would help me score a better part in the play. I met her in her small office, overcrowded with scripts, records, and costume fabric swatches.

I sat on the edge of my chair and explained my many years of dance experience. Mrs. Sharpp smiled at me from behind her ten pounds of caked-on makeup.

"You're a really good dancer, Melinda," she said, flashing me a red lipstick-stained smile. "It's just that...," she pursed her lips and thought for a moment, "...the chorus dancers do high kicks, and we really need all those kicks to be at the same height."

"Oh," I said. "I'm too short."

"You're very talented, Melinda. And you've got a great speaking voice. That's why you'll make an all-star telegram boy."

"Oh," I nodded like I got it, even though I didn't. "Okay, thanks for meeting with me." I grabbed my book bag and headed toward the door.

"Remember, there are no small roles," Mrs. Sharpp said dramatically and without a trace of irony, "only small actors."

♦ ♦ ♦

I told the story to Will as we trudged down Orchard Boulevard after school. Stan had stood us up for a ride.

"Are you gonna take the part?" Will asked.

"I don't know," I said. "It's not what I even auditioned for, but I don't want to seem like a sore loser."

"Yeah, be the bigger person." He paused. "You know what I mean."

I laughed, but I felt sad. "Why can't people stop focusing on my height?"

Will stopped and faced me. "It's not that people are focused on it—it's that you always bring it up."

"What do you mean?"

"You're, like, obsessed with it. People couldn't forget you're small if they tried."

"Really?" I asked. "In a bad way?"

"No, no," Will quickly answered. "But I can tell it bothers you."

We heard the honk of a horn as Stan pulled up. "Sorry," he yelled, rolling down the window. "I had to stay after in chem."

I started to head toward the car. Will grabbed my hand, slipping his finger between my wrist and charm bracelet. "Hey, Min, wait," he said. I turned around, looking up at him. "You've gotta realize that it's cool to be short. You're great just the way you are."

♦ ♦ ♦

Stan dropped Will off and then pulled into our driveway. I threw my book bag onto a kitchen chair and proceeded up to my room. My charm bracelet felt warm on my wrist, and I kept thinking about what Will had said: "*You're great just the way you are.*" And, I repeated it out loud. Then, my thoughts flipped to the way he smiled at me when he had gotten out of the car. It was not a "bye, Stan's little sister" smile. It was more.

I thought of what else Will had said: "*You always bring it up.*" Could it be possible that guys treat me like their kid sister because I treat them like big brothers?

Maybe I just need to get over this, I thought to myself as I yanked off my shoes. I sat on my bed and grabbed my pillow. The doctor told me I'm done growing, so I figured I might as well learn to like being short.

Besides, there must be some cool things about being short. I picked fuzz off my sweater, rolled it between my fingers, and thought of one of the benefits to being short: I always get a discount at the movies because they always assume I'm 12 or younger. Claudia and Lindy have to pay the student price, which is two bucks more. I can also curl up easily to read a book. I can move quickly in dance class.

Okay, I told myself, *maybe it's not always so bad being short.*

◆ ◆ ◆

The next day at lunch, I told Lindy and Claudia I had come up with a bunch of reasons that make me glad to be short.

"Tell me one," Claudia said between bites of her Caesar wrap.

I rested my fork inside my salad bowl. "I can still eat off the kids' menu at most restaurants," I said.

Lindy nodded. "Cool, very cool."

"Plus, I can stretch out all the way in the bathtub."

Claudia put down her wrap. "I wish I could do that, Min. My knees always stick up and freeze."

"*And*, I can lie down in the back seat of the car and sleep during family road trips," I added.

Lindy interrupted, "I envy that. I'm too tall and I have to sleep sitting up. It is *sooo* uncomfortable. You have no idea. I have to push my head against the window to get into a good position."

"You're lucky, Min," Claudia agreed.

"Plus, I can dance really fast in dance class."

"You really are a great dancer," Lindy admitted.

I thought for a moment and picked another "happy I'm short" reason: "My favorite jeans." Lindy and Claudia looked confused. "Since I've stopped growing, I can still wear my favorite jeans," I explained.

"The really soft ones with the perfect bottom fit?" Lindy asked. I nodded.

"You really do have a huge wardrobe," Claudia added.

I smiled. "Years of collecting."

"And," I said slowly, saving the best for last. "If I am to be

Tinkerbell, I get to have a Captain Hook."

Lindy patted her mouth with her napkin and then stuffed it into her brown lunch bag. "Don't you mean Peter Pan?" she asked, leaning forward. "He's the match for Tinkerbell."

"Oh, no," I explained, searching my salad for the last crunchy crouton. "The tights are a little too much. Captain Hook is much better."

Claudia perked up. "Where are you going with this, Minnie?" she asked, scooting her chair closer to the table.

"Will," I said secretively, popping my crouton bounty into my mouth and giving it a satisfying chomp, "is going to be my Captain Hook. He passed me a note asking me to the May Mixer."

Lindy shrieked. "When!?"

I pulled out the note and handed it over. "He gave it to me on the ride to school this morning."

Lindy devoured the note, reading it out loud for Claudia: *"I know the May Mixer is for the girls to ask the guys, but I think a Tinkerbell needs a Captain Hook to go with. What do you say?"*

Lindy looked at me with a smile. "This is *so* much better than a 'Dr. and Mrs. Tidmore' note from Louis," she announced. I laughed.

"Tell me you said you'll go with him," Claudia demanded.

"I'm telling him after school," I explained, pulling a note out of my back pocket and showing them. "I was going to give him this."

"Dear CH, I'd love to. Signed, Tink," Claudia read out loud.

Lindy grabbed the note and squinted so she could read my mini-sized Minnie handwriting. "Very cool," she said as she refolded the note. "I think you're going to have a really fun time."

"I think so, too," I said. "I make a really *great* Tinkerbell!"

♦ ♦ ♦

The Dog Formerly Known As Victor Maximilian Bonaparte Lincoln Rothbaum

Carolyn Mackler

It was bad enough when Meg's parents had a custody battle over her. Now they're back in court—this time over the family dog.

My life has hit an all-time low. My parents went to court today over custody of Victor Maximilian Bonaparte Lincoln Rothbaum. He's our 12-pound powder-puff pooch. He's a Bichon Frise. That's his breed, not a salad in some fancy French restaurant.

My parents got the dog to save their marriage. They had started arguing a lot about two years ago, so their marriage counselor suggested they find something they could learn about together. I thought maybe they'd take up birdwatching in Central Park or cross-country skiing.

But, no. They were all, "Meghan, we're getting a dog!"

I was in sixth grade at the time. When I heard "dog," I envisioned a golden retriever or a black Lab or even a mutt. We'd name it Otis or Booker or Scamp. I'd teach him to fetch sticks and catch Frisbees.

Two weeks later, my parents came home with a cottonball swaddled in a baby blanket. They named him Victor Maximilian Bonaparte Lincoln Rothbaum, after assorted historical figures (but, Rothbaum is our last name). And, they always insisted on calling him by his full name. He quickly grew on me, despite the five-names-in-one thing and the fact that he practically spent his life at the grooming salon, getting shampooed 'til his coat was as white as a bleached bone.

My big sister, Katy, was in college, two hours north of New York City. So, I was home alone most afternoons. That's when Victor Maximilian Bonaparte Lincoln Rothbaum and I bonded. I'd sit on the sofa, flipping channels, and he'd nuzzle in my lap and slurp my fingers. I'd toss his chew-toy to the other end of the couch and—surprise!— he'd carry it back to me.

After six months of toting the pup in an infant blankie and buying him miniature rain slickers, my parents were arguing again. It was worse than before. By the time I was in seventh grade, their marriage was going down the garbage chute faster than a bag of dog doo. And then last summer, they got divorced.

First off, they went to court over me, Meghan Rothbaum. Most everyone just calls me Meg. I'm 14 and in ninth grade now, but sometimes I feel like I'm about 40. Since my parents fight so much, I have to be the fair, rational one. My goal is to never stir up trouble.

After a grueling court battle that left me in tears almost every night, the judge granted my parents 50-50 custody. So, ever since, I spend one week in each apartment, switching on Sundays. I hate lugging my homework back and forth, and always having to remember what clothes are where and what bus I should take home from school and what I can and can't tell each parent. But—"adult" that I am—I don't want to make things worse by complaining.

After the custody decision, my parents were in court all fall, wrestling over everything else they owned—the apartment, the car, the set of chipped dishes, the photos from a Florida vacation when we all got so many mosquito bites we had to fly home three days early. But now, they are down to the last thing they have to fight over—Victor Maximilian Bonaparte Lincoln Rothbaum. Ever since they split last summer, my mom has kept him. Now my dad wants *his* turn.

Have I pointed out to them the absurdity of a custody battle over a dog? Nope. I just zip my lips and count the days until I can go to college to escape all this craziness.

♦ ♦ ♦

Day Two of the Rothbaum vs. Rothbaum Canine Custody Battle (I'll get to Day One in a sec). It's a Tuesday evening in early March. I'm staying at my mom's this week. I'm in the kitchen with her, eating Indian takeout from cartons and listening to her account of the courtroom drama. She's hacking apart her samosa as she describes how my dad brought in a witness who said he spotted my mom and Victor Maximilian Bonaparte Lincoln Rothbaum weaving through traffic as they dashed across 79th Street.

I wash down my veggie curry with a swig of lemonade. Last night on the phone, my dad told me how, on Day One, my mom told the judge that when they were potty-training Victor Maximilian Bonaparte Lincoln Rothbaum, my dad slapped the dog's nose for going to the bathroom on the kitchen floor. I listen to both sides, telling them it'll work out for the best.

As soon as my mom steps into the shower, I scoop up Victor Maximilian Bonaparte Lincoln Rothbaum, carry him into my room, and flip off the light. He squirms as we snuggle under the covers but, after I weave my fingers through his fluffy ears, he settles down.

Still holding him in one arm, I grab the phone from my bedside table. The buttons light up, so I can dial my sister Katy's number in the dark. She lives off campus, in a country house with four friends.

"Hello?" Katy's housemate answers.

I can never tell who's who, so I just say, "Hi. Is Katy there? This is her sister."

"Sure. Hang on a sec."

A minute later, Katy gets on the phone. "Hey, Meg! What's up?"

I feel like crying as soon as I hear my sister's voice. I tighten my elbow around Victor Maximilian Bonaparte Lincoln Rothbaum. He licks my collarbone.

"They're off the deep end," I say.

Katy groans. "What is it this time—the couch?"

"They fought over that in October."

"The books?"

"Nope," I say, "Dad got the non-fiction. Mom got the novels. That went down in December."

"What is it then?"

"It's Victor Maximilian Bonaparte Lincoln Rothbaum."

"Custody of the dog?" Katy asks.

"It's worse than the custody battle over me."

"Oh, no." Katy is quiet for a few seconds. Then, she says, "Meg, maybe the dog should come up to Poughkeepsie and live with me. I'm sure it would be fine with my housemates. And he'll have five happy parents, instead of two unhappy ones."

I don't say anything for a moment—just stare into the dark.

"What do you think?" Katy asks.

"I don't know, Katy. You know how they are. They'd freak."

"Do you want me to say something to them?"

I take a deep breath and let it out slowly. Fair and rational people don't go around making trouble. "No. Let's just leave it alone."

"At least think about it?" Katy asks.

Victor Maximilian Bonaparte Lincoln Rothbaum wriggles out of my arms and jumps to the floor. He trots over to the corner of my room, where I keep his toys and bones. I can hear him sinking his teeth into his squeaky shoe.

"Okay," I say. "I'll think about it."

♦ ♦ ♦

The Canine Custody Battle ends on Day Three. The judge rules that my parents must share Victor Maximilian Bonaparte Lincoln Rothbaum 50-50, just like they do with me. I'll bring him with me when I switch on Sundays.

Victor Maximilian Bonaparte Lincoln Rothbaum is anxious, antsy, and constantly gnawing his fur. My dad bought some chew-toys, but the dog never knows where they are. At my mom's, he keeps peeing on the throw rugs in the living room. He's totally stressed out.

By the third week, something in me just pops. My dad and I are on the couch watching a movie. Victor Maximilian Bonaparte Lincoln Rothbaum is flopped on the rug, chewing his hip. My face muscles are tight, and a headache is creeping into my temples. I glance at my dad. He looks relaxed, his head leaning against a pillow.

"Dad," I say, my voice shaking, "I need to talk to you."

My dad pauses the movie. "Everything okay, Meg?"

"No," I say. My eyes are stinging with tears. I rarely cry around my parents, not since they split up, but I can't stop myself. I'm not feeling very fair or rational just now.

I wipe my eyes and tell my dad how hard the one-week-here/one-week-there is for Victor Maximilian Bonaparte Lincoln Rothbaum. How a dog needs consistency, a stable home, routines. I even tell him about Katy's offer, to keep him at college with her.

"Maybe that's not such a bad idea," my dad says, totally surprising me. "Let me sleep on it, Meg."

When I get home from school the next afternoon, I call my mom at her office. All day, I've been working up the nerve to tell her the same thing I told my dad, to try to persuade her to rethink our dog's destiny.

Before I can launch into my prepared speech, my mom says, "I spoke with your father this morning. We're both glad you said what's on your mind. We agree that it's a good plan to send the dog up to Katy's, at least for the time being."

"You and Dad *agreed* on something?" I ask, nearly dropping the phone.

I can hear my mom close the door to her office. "I know it's been a hard year, Meg, but your father and I are going to try to get along better."

"For Victor Maximilian Bonaparte Lincoln Rothbaum's sake?" I ask.

"Actually," my mom says, "for *all* of our sakes." I burst into tears for the second day in a row.

◆ ◆ ◆

The following Saturday, my dad takes me to Grand Central Station. I'm taking a train up to Poughkeepsie with a friend of my sister's who is also visiting her for the day.

It's an easy ride up the Hudson River. I take the window seat. Victor Maximilian Bonaparte Lincoln Rothbaum is in his carrying case, poking his wet charcoal nose through the door. I hold the case on my lap. Down by my feet, I set the bag with his dish, bones, and seven chew-toys. But that's all. No frills. Earlier this morning, my mom and I packed up his blankie and his miniature rain slickers in a box and stowed them away in the hall closet.

Katy meets us at the train station. She gives me a bear hug and doesn't let go for a long time. Then, we hop into her car and drive to her house. It's an old farmhouse with a massive yard. Two of Katy's housemates are sitting on the front porch. When we pull in, they hop up, all waves and smiles.

I set the carrying case on the porch and unlatch it. Victor Maximilian Bonaparte Lincoln Rothbaum bounds down the porch steps. He charges across the yard and immediately digs a tiny hole, spraying dirt all over himself.

Katy's housemates go on and on about how cute he is and how he can dig all the holes he wants now that he's a country dog. Katy and I look at each other like, "Wow." This is the filthiest he's ever been in his entire life.

I fill Katy and her housemates in on what he eats, his favorite toys, and how frequently he needs to be brushed.

"What's his name again?" one of the housemates asks.

I glance at Katy.

"Vic," I say. "His name is simply Vic."

On the train ride home, I can't stop thinking about the dog formerly known as Victor Maximilian Bonaparte Lincoln Rothbaum. Before Katy drove her friend and me back to the train station, it took us 10 minutes to locate him so I could kiss him goodbye. One of Katy's housemates finally spotted him in the backyard, rolling in soggy leaves. He looked like he was having the time of his life. As I scratched his head, streaked with mud and grass stains, he licked my cheeks.

I stare out the train window at the wide, gray Hudson. I'm going to miss our little dog. I hope we made the right decision, bringing him up here.

The train zips up a fast incline. I open and close my mouth to unclog my ears. That's when it dawns on me. I haven't felt like an adult these past few days. I've felt a little sad, but also goofy and free. I've felt 14.

Maybe this is going to be good for all of us—this change of pace, the end of one way of life and the beginning of another. Sure, it's unknown, but it's got to be better than before. It's time to start over. For me, for my mom, for my dad, even for Victor Maximilian Bonaparte Lincoln Rothbaum—also known as just Vic.

The Invisible Boy

Wendy Mass

Sometimes, you have to make like you're invisible for people to actually see you for the first time.

I was six weeks old before my parents named me. You'd think it wouldn't have taken them so long to come up with Harry.

My mother was nearly 40 when I was born, so my parents originally called me Gift, as in "our little gift from heaven." Luckily, my grandma convinced my mother she couldn't name a kid Gift, so they chose Harry, after my deceased grandfather. They tell me my grandfather was a great guy and all, but I could have done without hearing "Hairy Harry" every day of first grade.

But now, because of the whole Harry Potter-fest, my name is suddenly cool and I don't mind it so much. Not that I want to be a wizard or anything, but I sure wouldn't mind having his invisibility cloak. Boy, if you could get those from Silverman's Cash 'n' Carry, I'd be the first person in line. Believe me, you'd want to be invisible if you were me.

It all began when I was eight months old and miraculously started speaking in nearly full sentences. "Oh my word!" my mother yelled upon hearing me say, "No more pink juice. Hate pink juice."

"He's a prodigy," my father confirmed, grinning broadly. "We always knew he was destined for greatness."

From that day on, not only was I "a little gift from heaven," I was a certified genius in their eyes. It didn't seem to matter that by the time I was six, I wasn't much brighter than any other kid in the first grade.

Now that I'm in seventh grade, I don't even make honor roll. My parents have yet to accept that I peaked early and fizzled out. They still expect greatness and fully trust that my genius will re-emerge in plenty of time to get me into Harvard.

At breakfast, the newspaper is neatly arranged next to my cereal bowl with certain articles circled, courtesy of my father. Every time I come home from school, they grill me about what I learned that day. And dinners usually go something like this:

Dad (in between bites of brisket): "Capitol of Argentina?"

Me: "I don't remember."

Mom: "C'mon, Honey, we went over this last night."

Me (sighing loudly): "Buenos Aires."

Mom and Dad then clap and mark off the answer in their notebook. Every time I fill a page with correct answers, I get a treat. I'm like a dog being trained not to wet on the rug. I wish my parents would get a hobby, like croquet or checkers—a hobby other than me, because I can't breathe.

The only place I get any peace is in the bathtub, which is where I am now. I know most kids my age take showers at the end of the day, but most kids don't have my parents. I wait until my skin is pruned and puckered before getting out of the tub. I put my school clothes back on and quietly sneak out the front door. My parents are in the den watching *Jeopardy* and taking notes for future dinner quizzes, so I know they won't notice I'm gone until at least the first commercial.

It's 7 p.m. and, since it's spring, the sun hasn't totally set yet. This is my favorite time of day—not yet night, but not day, either. The air seems thick with possibilities. I sit on the curb in front of our house and rest my head on my knees. Ten glorious no-parent minutes pass before I feel a tap on my shoulder. I look up, surprised to see someone other than a parental unit.

It's Rob Green, who lives across the street. We used to build Lego fortresses together until he started high school and became too cool for Legos—and me. His younger sister, Lizzy, is in my grade. Their father moved away last year to one of the square-shaped states, but I can never remember which one. Now, Rob has to keep Lizzy out of trouble. Rumor has it that she stole some candy from Silverman's Cash 'n' Carry, and Rob made her give it back.

"Hey, everything okay?" Rob asks.

"Uh, I guess so."

"You look like a guy with a problem."

I nod. "My folks, if you must know."

"They ignore you, right?" he says, kicking at the dirt in the street with the heel of his sneaker. "Like you're invisible or something."

"I wish!" I confess. "My parents pay too much attention to me. It's driving me nuts. No matter where I go or what I do, they find me."

"If you really want to change things," Rob says, "I can help you."

"Really? How?"

"I can teach you how to make yourself invisible."

He must be kidding, I'm thinking, but his expression is dead serious. "Just come over after school tomorrow," he says.

With that, he takes off across the street and disappears behind his front door. I catch a glimpse of Lizzy through their living room window, and I get sick to my stomach. I have a feeling she heard the whole conversation—but no, she couldn't have from so far away. It's bad enough that, every time I see her, I'm reminded of the time she laughed at me when I kissed her at Amy Levine's spin-the-bottle party in fifth grade. But if Rob's plan works, I won't have to worry about Lizzy laughing at me anymore.

♦ ♦ ♦

On the bus after school the next day, Lizzy plops down next to me and shoves a stick of gum in her mouth. I consider pointing out the big No GUM OR FOOD sign the driver taped above the rearview mirror, but what's the use? I stare out the window instead.

After a few minutes of blissful silence, she says, "So you're letting my brother help you? He couldn't even tie his shoes until he was 10!"

I'm about to tell her to mind her own biz when I get a whiff of her shampoo. I recognize the flowery smell from when I kissed her at that ill-fated party. I feel my face heat up and quickly turn back to the window. I watch her from the corner of my eye as she lazily draws a butterfly on her jeans with a black pen.

Fifteen minutes later, the bus drops us off at our block. That morning, I'd told my mother I was taking the later bus so I could stay at school and finish a bio project. I figure that buys me an hour or so.

I walk the long way around the block so I don't have to pass my house and risk being seen. I ring Rob's doorbell, and Lizzy opens the door.

"He's not home yet," she says, blowing a big bubble and letting her gum pop all over her lips. She expertly peels it off and says, "Come on in."

"I'll just wait out here," I tell her, sitting down on the top porch step.

"Suit yourself," she says, closing the door harder than necessary.

Rob's friend drops him off five minutes later. "You could have waited inside. Lizzy's probably home."

"That's okay." I follow him in.

"She scares you, huh?" Rob says, tossing his backpack on the stairs.

"A little," I admit.

"She's harmless," Rob says. "As long as you don't get on her bad side, that is."

I glance around to make sure she's not in earshot. "She has a *good* side?"

He laughs. The first thing I see when he opens the door to his room is a colorful poster that takes up a quarter of the wall. It wasn't there during our Lego days.

"That's a Sri Yantra diagram," Rob explains. "The interconnecting triangles are supposed to lead you into a sort of hypnotic state so you can travel through time. I'll use it as part of our training."

"Training?"

"Dude, you don't flip on a switch and, bam, you're invisible. It takes training. Like Daniel and Mr. Miyagi."

"Who?"

"Haven't you seen *The Karate Kid*?"

I shake my head.

He stares in amazement. "It's a movie on cable, like, every day."

I shrug. "My mother won't let me watch movies that aren't G-rated until I start high school."

"Geez," he says, shaking his head. "We're going to have to move fast." He spreads some books out on the floor.

I lean over and glance at the titles—*The Dummy's Guide to Mysticism; The Holographic Universe;* and *New Physics: It's Not Your Father's Physics.*

"Did you read all these?" I ask.

"Twice! And in order to become invisible, you've gotta understand the nature of reality. Now, you know there's no such thing as objective reality, right?"

I nod, but I'm really thinking, "*Huh*?"

"Everything we think we know is really only perceived by our senses. The sounds we hear are just waves in the air; colors are electromagnetic radiation. Your sense of taste comes from molecules that match a specific area on your tongue. Hey, if our eyes could access the infrared part of the light spectrum, the sky would be green and trees would be red. So in reality, no one really knows the color of the sky or trees. Get it?"

I nod again. But I don't get it.

"Matter is a wave of energy, and the molecules that make up our bodies are actually everywhere and nowhere at the same time. When you realize you're just a wave of energy, you can disappear," he adds, confusing me further.

My eyes widen. "When do I start?"

"Right now," Rob says. "Stand about a foot in front of the poster. Stare directly at the center of the design, but relax your eyes so they kind of cross a little. Nod when you've got it."

I try to relax my eyes but, each time I do, they start to close. Finally, I just look at the poster like I'm looking at something much farther away, and it seems to work. I nod to Rob.

"Great," he says. "Now visualize a white light, and imagine yourself inside that light. The white light is getting really bright. It's starting to absorb the objects in my room."

"It is?" I ask.

"Yes. No talking! Now, see yourself getting blurry from inside the light until you can't see the light anymore."

My head gets lighter as I imagine the white light around me. It's like the whole world is within that poster and the edges of the design start to fade.

"Is it working? Am I invisible?"

Rob shakes his head. "Nope. I can still see you."

I sigh and reluctantly turn away from the poster. "How long did it take you to be able to do it?"

"Me? I've never actually tried it."

I stare at him, suspiciously.

"Hey, I never said *I* could do it. I just said I could teach *you* how."

"I bet you never read those books, either!"

He shrugged. "Read, skimmed, browsed—same difference."

With one last glare, I leave his room and almost trip racing down the stairs.

Rob follows me. "Why would I ever need to be invisible? I'm popular, and my mom never bugs me. I can do whatever I want," he says.

"Good for you!" I shout back.

"Don't give up, Harry," he says as I swing the screen door open.

I almost trip over Lizzy, who's perched on the bottom step of the porch like a lawn decoration. "Yeah, Harry," she says. "Don't give up."

I ignore her and walk quickly across the lawn. She keeps up with me.

"Seriously, Harry. Just tell your parents you need some privacy. They follow you all over the house."

I whirl around. "How would *you* know that?"

She points to the many windows of my house facing the street. "You never pull the shades down."

I don't have the energy to be furious at her. This day just keeps getting worse.

"Hang in there," she says, reaching up and patting me on the shoulder. "You're not that bad of a guy."

"Gee, thanks, Lizzy. Coming from you, that means a whole lotta nothing."

"Hmmph," she says, pivoting and turning back toward her house. "If you want to be invisible, you should have asked me, not Rob."

I watch her walk away, and then I storm into my house and pull down the shades on every window.

"What are you doing?" my mother asks as I cross the living room.

"Did you know the neighbors can see inside our house?"

"No one's looking inside our house, Harry," she says, raising the shades.

I open my mouth to tell her she's wrong, but I realize I'd have to explain about Lizzy and the whole invisibility thing, and that would ruin everything. They'd probably never let me leave the house again.

A few hours later, I'm in my room doing homework, shade pulled securely down, when my dad hands me a carefully folded note with my name on it.

"I found this on the porch," he says. "Who is it from?"

"I don't know." I turn it over in my hand. It looks like those notes girls always pass to each other during class when they think the teacher isn't looking. I unfold it and smooth it out on top of my desk: *"Even though you said you don't need my help, I think you do. Meet me at the brook behind the painted rock at 3:00 tomorrow. Lizzy."*

I whisk the note off my desk before my dad can read it. "It's just something from school," I tell him. He looks at me sideways but, surprisingly, leaves the room without pressing me for more info. I don't know how to feel about the note. Angry? Excited? Embarrassed? By the time I get into bed (after reading the note five more times), I decide on a combination of all three.

♦ ♦ ♦

Even though I have a nagging feeling nothing good could possibly come of it, at 2:45 the next day, I duck through the hole in the fence that leads to the brook. Just as I'm almost all the way through, I snag my sleeve on a nail so it rips just enough that it'll be hard to explain to my mother.

"It's about time," Lizzy says.

I climb down the rocks and join her by the edge of the water. I hold up my left wrist. "It's not even three o'clock yet."

She shakes her head. "No, I mean being invisible is about time."

"Huh?"

"It's all about knowing how to slow down time," she says, dipping one sandaled toe into the water. "Just do what I tell you, and you'll get it."

"Hold on there. Before I agree to anything, tell me something— have you ever been invisible?"

"Um, nice rip in your shirt. I think it's getting bigger."

She's right—it *is* getting bigger. "I'm hoping my mother won't notice," I tell her. "And stop changing the subject!"

"No, I've never done it myself. But that doesn't mean..."

I shake my head and scramble back up the rocks. "I'm so outta here!"

"Wait, Harry, just listen for five minutes. That's all I ask."

I'm about to tell her she has two minutes and that's it, but the sun is glinting off her hair and her skin looks all smooth and sparkly and my words get completely caught up in my throat. Suddenly, my left heel slips on a rock, and I feel myself going down. Lizzy tries to grab me, but it's too late. My right leg twists around and I land hard. The pain is sharp, and it knocks the wind out of me. I force myself to look down. My foot is sticking out in the way-wrong direction. The thing I hear before everything gets dark is Lizzy saying, "Your mom's gonna notice that."

♦ ♦ ♦

According to this week's vocabulary list—which my mother picked up for me along with the rest of my homework—I'm now "deficient," which means: lacking something essential; incomplete or defective. My ankle is broken, and I have to walk with crutches and wear a cast. And, I can't scratch the constant itch of my covered skin.

"Are you comfortable?" my mother asks, straightening the pile of pillows under my right leg.

"I guess," I say, even though I'm not.

"Good. Ring the bell if you need anything. I'll be downstairs in the kitchen," she says, then slowly backs out of the room, closing the door behind her. Right now, Dad is outside planting shrubs. If I lean up and turn my head really far to the right, I can see him. For the first time ever, he hasn't asked for my help in the yard. I mean, I could have sat on a chair and handed him the gardening tools or something.

♦ ♦ ♦

I must have dozed off because I'm startled to see my mother standing over my bed looking at me with what I can only describe as surprise. Sort of like she is really seeing me for the first time. "This arrived while you were sleeping," she says. She hands me a note that looks identical to the last one and waits patiently for me to open it.

"Um, can I have some privacy, please?" I've never said those words to her before. They hang in the air like deflating helium balloons.

My mother takes a step back. "Oh…of course," she says, closing the door softly behind her. I don't hear her footsteps heading down the hall yet, but it's progress.

I quickly unfold the note and read: "*Dear Harry, I tried baking chocolate chip cookies, but it turns out I'm not cut out for the kitchen. I'm sorry you got hurt. And not just your ankle. I'm sorry I laughed when you kissed me at Amy's party. I was not laughing at you; I was just nervous. But I know it didn't come off that way. I hope you get better. That's it. That's all I have to say. I know it's not much. Lizzy.*"

She's wrong. It's a lot.

At this moment, it's *everything*.

The Anonymous Birthday Club

Mary Grace Joseph, age 13

A major mistake turns into a birthday party
Tori and her friends don't soon forget!

"H appy Birthday, Tori!" my friends shouted. It was Tuesday, March 22nd and nowhere near my birthday. To say the least, I was shocked.

"What is this?" I asked everyone.

I looked around the room. There was Molly, redheaded and feisty as ever, but a doll; Mia, my spunky neighbor; Caroline, the all-time Monopoly champ; and Randi, with bracelets galore, as usual.

"It's your birthday, silly! And since you didn't invite us to your party, we decided to invite ourselves," Caroline said for them all.

"Thanks guys, but it's not my birthday." I said. Their faces fell. "My birthday is October 19th."

"How were we so far off?" Mia asked with a scowl directed at Randi.

Randi's face became rosy red. "Sorry, Tori. I guess I kinda forgot. But today is *someone's* birthday." She perked up at the thought.

"Duh! It's somebody's birthday. There's like how many billion people that live on this earth?" Molly said between mouthfuls of Cheetos.

Caroline tossed me a bag of chips and I gladly dug into them.

Pause.

Let me give you the scene: It was a crisp, spring day, and I had walked home from school. There my friends were, munching on my food...and thankfully letting me have some!

So that's how it all began: The Anonymous Birthday Club. Once a week, we would get together and celebrate somebody's birthday, though we didn't know who we were celebrating for. Every once in a while, we would know someone having a birthday and then have a double bash.

It was kinda crazy, but it was mostly just an excuse for the five of us to get together, have fun, and eat junk food. Plus, we got to decorate. We'd hang crépe paper, balloons, and a humongous 'Happy Birthday' sign in the rec room of my house. I tried to convince my friends that we should take turns hosting the parties, but they loved my oversized game room too much. Oh well, at least I'm loyal.

When October 19th finally rolled around, I was majorly ready for it. I had a giant party (with lots of crépe paper!). I invited all of the Birthday Club and some other friends, too. It was totally the best party the whole Birthday Club had ever thrown.

Mia, Molly, and Caroline came home from school with me one day after that. Randi had a dentist appointment or something. We were decorating for yet another birthday.

"Could you please pass the crépe paper, Caroline?" Molly asked in a way-too-polite-tone that we all knew to ignore.

"Uh, let me try to find it." Caroline dug around the game room.

Here's the scene: *hectic.* Glue, paper, scissors, and little bits of everything strewn across the floor. Mia, making an additional "Happy Birthday" sign. Me, getting lightheaded from blowing up balloons. Molly, up on a configuration of tables and chairs trying to reach my ceiling to hang balloons from it. And Caroline, scurrying around through us all, trying to meet Molly's every demand.

That's when reality hit us. All at the same time. I ran out of balloons and Molly just had to have more, so I scoured the house for some. Nope, all out. Caroline informed me that the crépe paper was totally and completely gone as well. Well, I informed her that was all we had. Mia messed up on the sign and wanted to know if I had any more poster board. I was ready to scream, but calmly told her, "No!"

Reality hit Molly hardest…literally. She came crashing down from her little mountain of chairs, hit her elbow hard, and scraped her knee. She was wailing. I was ready to. This was just too much! This was it. We had used up all of our pooled supplies. Just then, in the peak of our aggravation, Randi walked in cool and pulled together.

"Hey guys, how's it going?" She smiled her sincere Randi smile.

We all just stared blankly at her.

"Okay, okay, I get it," she said. "Sorry, guys." That's what I love about Randi, she understands everything, whether it's in words, or not. Like now.

I have no idea why, but at that moment, Randi started laughing hysterically. It probably was pretty funny. Molly on the floor, and the rest of us gathered around her, buried in scraps of paper. Then, suddenly, we all erupted in laughter. By the time we stopped laughing, we were all on the floor rolling, right beside Molly.

Then and there, we held an Anonymous Birthday Club meeting. We decided to stop the balloon thing, stop the sign thing, and definitely stop the crépe paper thing. All we would have at our weekly parties were food and friends. Which, I later decided, are definitely the two most important parts of a party, anyway—except on the days of our own real birthdays.

Confessions of a Movie Star Extra

Carolyn Mackler

When Saffron gets cast as an extra in a movie, it's her first step on the road to stardom. That is, until Saffron figures out that fame isn't all it's cracked up to be.

WEDNESDAY, JUNE 18

2:19 p.m.

Six minutes into summer vacation and it already stinks. I'm sweating bullets as I dump the contents of my locker into a Hefty bag. My best friend just hugged me goodbye because her parents are meeting her in front of the school so they can drive her to the airport and put her on a plane to Costa Rica. She's spending the summer rehabilitating monkeys for an organization called Kids Saving the Rainforest. The only monkey I'm going to see this summer is my mom's new boyfriend. They're both lawyers, and they met through work about three months ago. My mom is so nuts over him she can't even see that his ears stick out and his eyes are closely set. If I knew the phone number of an anthropologist, I would totally call because this guy is the missing link between humans and primates.

2:22 p.m.

That's another reason this summer is going to stink. When my mom isn't working, she's out with the Missing Link, so she won't be around to drive me to the movies. You name it—chick flicks, knee-slappers, tear-jerkers—I need my fix of Hollywood glitz. But scrap that idea, because I'm only thirteen and nowhere near being able to drive, so anything I do has to be within hoofing distance.

I know it sounds crazy, but when I sit in the dark theater and watch all those movies, I can totally picture myself on the screen. Yes, me. Saffron Jones: future star. Presently stuck in Brockport for the summer with a missing best friend, a missing mom, and the Missing Link.

2:29 p.m.

Just as I'm chucking the last of the crumpled-up gum wrappers from the depths of my locker, I spot Mr. O'Malley walking down the hall, going, "Saffron! I'm glad I caught you."

Big-time *oh*, big-time *no*. Mr. O'Malley is my English teacher. I bet he's going to inform me that I flubbed the final and will have to take summer school. I am so totally doomed.

2:47 p.m.

I am so totally excited. I'm in the bathroom, washing the locker grime off my face and applying lip gloss. It's a tube of Wet 'n' Wild that I found in my locker. I'm not even sure it ever belonged to me. But movie stars are never seen without their lip gloss, so this will have to do.

Yes, MOVIE STARS!!!

I did not bomb English, or at least not that I know of yet. When Mr. O'Malley approached me, he was all, "Are you auditioning?"

I wasn't too surprised to hear him say that because, along with being an English teacher, Mr. O'Malley directs the school plays. This spring, I had a lead role in the school's musical. The whole time I was onstage I kept thinking about how someday, when I'm a celebrity and *E!* is interviewing me about my early acting roles, I'll be able to reminisce about middle school musicals.

Back to Mr. O'Malley. I tossed some gum wrappers into the trash and said, "I didn't know there was a school play this summer."

"Not a play, Saffron. *A movie.*"

"Huh?"

My English teacher proceeded to explain how a movie was going to be filmed in Brockport, next Monday and Tuesday. Not an entire movie, of course. Just a little bit of one, where the main character has flashbacks to his high school days. The director grew up in western New York, so when they were scouting for a small town, she pointed them our way.

"You'd better hurry up," Mr. O'Malley said. "Auditions are in the gym at 3:15."

"Auditions?"

"They're casting local teens as extras. Football players, cheerleaders. No speaking parts, and it doesn't pay, but it'll be lots of—"

Before he could finish, I was sprinting toward the nearest bathroom, clutching the lip gloss.

4:43 p.m.

I had arrived in the gym at 3:05, but it was already crammed. There are boys on one side, girls on the other. I join a fellow classmate, Mina, at the end of the girls' line, and we crane our necks to see what is happening up front.

There is one woman and one man sitting at a mystery-meat-encrusted table that they must have kidnapped from the cafeteria. The woman tells each girl to do a short cheer, and then the guy asks her a few questions about herself. I don't have any pom-pom experience, so Mina shows me a routine she knows from cheerleading.

4:51 p.m.

A middle-aged guy with a stringy ponytail announces into a megaphone that they're only casting twelve cheerleaders and twelve football players. But anyone who doesn't get selected for an extra-special extra role is encouraged to come by on Monday and Tuesday because they're going to need bodies to fill up the bleachers.

Mina tugs anxiously at my arm. "That's going to be us."

"You never know," I say.

But I do know. If this is my shot at making it big, nothing is going to stop me. I lick my lips for the hundredth time. My lip gloss is totally faded by now. *Oh, well.* I guess my inner stardom will have to shine through.

5:47 p.m.

We reach the front of the line. Mina goes first. Her cheering routine is perfect, but when they ask her why she'd be good for this movie, she freezes up. I try to smile at her, but she's staring at her sandals, mumbling monosyllabic answers. Finally, they're like, "Thank you very much" and then it's my turn.

I screw up once during the cheering routine, where I slap my thighs rather than clap my hands together as I'm spelling out S-P-I-R-I-T. But I smile with all twenty-eight teeth and do my best *Bring It On* spirit fingers. My enthusiasm works because, when I finish the cheer, the casting people are both grinning.

"So," the guy asks, "your name is Saffron? As in, the spice?"

I totally ham it up as I explain how my mom named me after the super-expensive, egg-yolk-yellow spice that's used in Spanish dishes like paella.

"It's a good conversation starter," I say. "And a great excuse to have expensive taste."

They both laugh. Then, the guy gives me the "hold on" signal with his hand and turns to chat with the woman.

I glance sideways. Mina is smiling at me and clutching her hands hopefully.

After what feels like forever, the woman says, "We'd like you to be a cheerleading extra in our movie. Please report to the stadium on Monday morning at nine o'clock."

"Saffron Jones," the guy adds in this dramatic voice. "Welcome to Hollywood."

5:58 p.m.
Omigosh!

5:58 p.m. and ten seconds
Oh. My. Gosh.

5:58 p.m. and fourteen seconds
I just got cast in a movie! I'm going to be famous! I never thought it would happen this early in my life. Or that Hollywood would find me, right here in boring old Brockport. I'm going to be a movie star. No, wait. I *am* a movie star!

SATURDAY, JUNE 21
9:43 a.m.
My mom and the Missing Link are going into Rochester today. He's picking her up shortly, so she's yanking sundresses out of her closet and modeling each option in front of the mirror. I'm hoping she'll finish getting dressed soon because I still need her to sign my permission form. After I got cast in the movie, the guy with the

stringy ponytail handed me a legal-looking paper and explained how I needed a parent to give a signature in order for them to film me.

But, my mom got home from work late on Wednesday night. And on Thursday and Friday nights, she was out with the Missing Link, so she still hasn't had a chance to sign it. But filming starts in about forty-seven hours, so I'm getting desperate.

It's strange. A few months ago, my mom would have signed the permission form in a heartbeat. That's how it used to be with us, ever since my dad took off five years ago. After that, my mom's world pretty much revolved around me. Whenever I did even the smallest thing, like get a star on a book report, she took me out for an ice-cream sundae to celebrate. But now, I'm a real star and she's too preoccupied with the Missing Link to even notice.

10:10 a.m.

The Missing Link just came into the kitchen, where I'm sitting at the table spooning Apple Jacks into my mouth. My mom is doing her makeup in the bathroom, so he leans against the counter and asks me, "How's it going?"

I tell him I've been cast in a movie. Perfect timing, because just then, my mom enters stage left. I hold the permission form under her nose until she dons her reading glasses, scans the paper, and scribbles her signature.

My movie star career has launched!

MONDAY, JUNE 23
11:01 a.m.

I'm learning that filming a movie is mostly about waiting around. I had left my house at 7:40 and hoofed it over to the stadium, arriving at 8:00. A half-hour later, the cheerleading coach showed up. She explained how they asked her to oversee the cheerleading extras, which she agreed to do without pay, in the hopes of meeting someone famous. Then, she ran into the key grip guy in the grocery store yesterday and he informed her that there are no celebrities in the cast and it's a low-budget movie that will probably never make it to the theaters. But I wouldn't let that get me down. I mean, who even knows what the key grip does?

Around 9:00, the other cheerleading extras trickled in. Eleven high school girls, all hailing from the varsity squad. I silently thanked my mom for naming me Saffron. I'm sure that's what gave me an edge during my audition. It always gets people to pay attention. And it's a funny story, especially when I tell people how, since that particular spice costs $500 a pound and I weigh 109, my market value is $54,500.

The squad taught me one of their standard cheers, with the coach on hand to offer pointers. We practiced for two hours, as the film crew lazed around eating bagels and drinking coffee, and the actors—none of whom I recognized—got their makeup done. The coach passed out skirts and sweaters for us to wear. Nothing special. Just the Brockport High School blue-and-white cheerleading outfits. I guess this really is a low-budget flick.

11:23 a.m.
The guy with the stringy ponytail gets on his megaphone and tells everyone that filming is going to begin very, very, very soon. I reach over and pick up my blue-and-white pom-poms. No one else stirs.

12:57 p.m.
Whenever they show a film set on *Entertainment Tonight*, you always see a wall of floodlights and a million cameras capturing the actors from all angles. So far, I haven't seen any additional lighting and there's only one camera. I overheard some guy saying it's because we're shooting digital, like it's supposed to be some great new thing. What it really means is that it's just a hand-held camera that resembles the camcorder my mom uses to film my dance recitals and school plays.

For the past hour, they've been repeating one scene over and over, where the Main Guy hands the Main Girl a ring and she chucks it in the grass and starts bawling. I don't know why they keep doing it again. It looked fine on the first take. And the second take. And the third take. Ring, chuck, bawl, cut. Ring, chuck, bawl, cut. How can you screw that up?

12:58 p.m.

Come to think of it, it doesn't look fine. It looks cheesy. Who tosses jewelry on the ground and starts crying? *Duh.*

1:29 p.m.

I head over to the school and buy a Snickers and a Coke from the vending machine. I'm walking back to the stadium when I spot Mr. O'Malley up in the bleachers. He waves me toward him. As I walk up the metal steps, he congratulates me on getting cast as a cheerleading extra. Then, he congratulates me on getting a B+ on the English final.

I never thought I'd say this, but I'm actually more excited about passing English than being cast in the movie.

3:40 p.m.

I'm thirsty and hungry and bored and counting the minutes until I can go home and take a shower.

3:42 p.m.

Still counting the minutes. It's been two since the last time I checked.

3:51 p.m.

Guess who's walking toward me? Mina! Carrying a carton of lemonade, some paper cups, and a box of Oreos.

"Just thought I'd stop by and see your debut," she says as she holds up the treats. "Also, I want to ensure that you'll remember me when you're a big star."

I thank her profusely and chug two cups of lemonade. "How did you get here?"

"My older brother drove me. He's parking the car."

I split apart an Oreo, scrape off the white filling with my bottom teeth, and say, "I didn't know you had an older brother."

3:57 p.m.

How could I *not* have known that Mina has an older brother? Oh. My. Gorgeous. His name is Randall. He's sixteen and has a cute smile.

Mina invites me to swim in their pool on Wednesday.

More smiles. More Oreos. Another glass of lemonade. Maybe this summer won't be so bad after all.

4:19 p.m.
The Stringy Ponytail Guy announces into his megaphone that the cheerleaders should get ready because we're on very, very, very soon. We all squeal and bounce around. They don't send the makeup artist our way, so we check each other's ponytails and make sure no one has lip gloss on her teeth.

5:05 p.m.
The cheerleaders aren't even in the foreground. We're just hooting off to one side as the Main Guy—dressed in football padding—lifts the Main Girl over his head and spins her in circles until it looks like they're both going to puke. It's even cheesier than the ring-chucking scene. I slap my thighs and shout until my throat is dry and my legs start to bruise.

6:16 p.m.
After twelve takes, the camera woman finally says, "Okay, I think we got it. See you girls tomorrow."

She doesn't even thank us. Neither does the director or Ponytail Guy. Ten hours of simmering in the hot sun, and they can't even spare us some gratitude? Welcome to Hollywood. I'm just reconsidering whether I want to be a movie star after all, when I glance up and I'm totally surprised.

My mom is smiling and walking toward me. She's holding the camcorder in one hand. Her other hand is intertwined with the Missing Link's.

"You look adorable in that cheerleading outfit," she says. "I got some great shots of you out there."

"When did you get here?" I croak. My throat is parched and tired.

"We've been in the bleachers over an hour," my mom says. "We left work early so we could see you getting filmed."

The Missing Link asks if he can get me something to drink. I point him in the direction of the vending machines and tell him a Coke would be great.

As soon as he's gone, I'm like, "You didn't tell me you'd be here today."

"Are you kidding? I wouldn't miss this for the world." My mom sets the camera in the grass and gives me a hug, even though I'm disgustingly sweaty and she's in a nice suit. "I'm sorry I haven't been around that much lately," she says.

"That's okay," I say. "The Missing, I mean, Arthur seems nice."

"He is, Saffron. He really is."

I'm not sure whether this is good news or bad. I want my mom to be happy, so I guess it's good. Clearly, I'm going to be seeing a lot more of the Missing Link. I may even have to stop thinking of him as an escaped zoo animal.

When my mom lets go of me, I say, "I'm totally grimy, but will you and Arthur take me out for ice cream?"

"We'd love to," my mom says. "To celebrate your first day as a movie star."

"I am so not a movie star." I groan, "Try, a lowly extra."

"To me," she says as she kisses my forehead, "you are *always* a star."

♦ ♦ ♦

How to Catch a Dog Food Snatcher

Laura Purdie Salas

*What can Tracy do when the family hound's chow is
disappearing and Mom's convinced she's the thief?
Find the real culprit, of course.*

Mom didn't believe me. As usual. "You just never know when to stop," she said, adjusting her rose-covered barrette and then bending down to adjust my three-year-old sister Victoria's matching one.

I do so know when to stop, I thought. *Right after it's funny and right before I get in trouble for it.* In this case, though, I hadn't even *done* it.

Steal dog food, that is. *Please.* Chester, our dog, is a sweetheart. Why on earth would I take my beloved chocolate lab Chester's food? Am I desperate to make kibble earrings for the craft fair next month?

"This is another unfunny joke, Tracy," Mom said.

My five-year-old brother, Nathan, padded between us and disappeared into the bathroom with peanut butter and twine. *Uh oh.* Time for one of his "scientrific spearmints."

I put down my pencil. Any reason's a good reason to avoid geometry. "Maybe if you're a cat, stealing dog food is funny. But *me*, steal dog food? That's just sad."

But someone *was* taking the food. Chester had sat by his bowl and howled off and on for three days before Mom finally realized his food was disappearing. She thought he was just being piggy. Poor Chester. Mom didn't believe him, either.

But Mom was convinced it was me, even though I swore I didn't do it. How unfair was that?

That night, Mom planned to watch Chester eat, but he is *soooo* slow. I poured half a cup of Doggy Do-Rights in his bowl.

"Chester!" I called. "Yummy treats. Come eat your Do-Rights."

He padded in, sniffed his bowl, and ate about four bits. Then, he disappeared to digest it. Honestly, if someone were stealing my food, you can bet I'd scarf it down. But not Chester. Grandma says Chester eats as slow as my Grandpa jogs. And if you ever saw my Grandpa jog, you'd know that's pretty slow.

Then, Mom got distracted by Victoria. My little sister is the kind of daughter mothers dream of, apparently. She loves lace and ruffles and even frilly hats. One time, she and Mom came to school to eat lunch with me, and they wore matching ruffled denim dresses. I wanted to dive under my plate of nachos and hide.

Anyway, Victoria wanted to "do" Mom's hair, so Mom sat on Victoria's bedroom floor while Victoria twirled around and stuck combs and barrettes on Mom's head.

"Almost done!" she chirped.

Nathan was playing Legos in the living room, and I stretched out on the couch to study geometry.

"Don't look," cried Nathan.

"I'm *not* looking," I said. "I'm just doing my homework. See?" I waved my geometry book.

"Mom!" he shrieked. "Tracy won't leave me alone. I'm building a secret fort, and she's spying on me."

Big sigh. "Tracy…"

"I'm going," I grumbled. I took my geometry book into my room.

Twenty minutes later, Chester began howling. We all went into the kitchen and stared at his empty food bowl.

Mom was ticked. "Tracy, this is just not funny anymore."

"It never *was* funny," I said. "That's how you know I didn't do it."

I needed to solve the mystery of the missing Doggy Do-Rights before Mom decided *I* had to be put on a leash.

I put my brain to work. What if *nobody* was stealing the dog food? Where could it be? Maybe Victoria accidentally twirled into the bowl and they spilled out. She might have thrown them away so Mom wouldn't yell. Not that Mom would ever get mad at her.

I took the lid off the trash can and picked through it. *Eeeuww.* Paper towels drenched with salad dressing, two days' worth of junk mail, leftover spaghetti, and lots of other nasty stuff. But no Doggy Do-Rights. Just a hovering smell.

Where else could the food be?

In science, we learned that an ant can carry twenty times its body weight. Maybe bugs were carrying off the food. Mom was insulted, but I searched the entire kitchen. Not a single, solitary ant.

My last idea was to search through Nathan's science drawer, where he keeps all sorts of disgusting things. I pawed through four dead marigolds, one dead goldfish (had Mom *ever* looked in here?), and seventeen rocks.

Mom stuck her head in the doorway and said, "Quit trying to get Nathan in trouble. He wouldn't take Chester's food."

And *I* would?! It was time for Plan B—the stakeout.

◆ ◆ ◆

The next morning, I half hid inside the damp, cramped cabinet under the sink.

I had been inside an endless hour, watching Chester nibble half-heartedly at his food. Suddenly, Victoria pranced into the kitchen. She lifted up the skirt of her velvet dress like an apron—and dumped the dog food into it! I was so stunned to see Her Delicate Royal Highness stealing dog food that I couldn't speak. She left the room.

I snuck out of the cabinet and stretched. What could she be doing? Building a castle? Feeding dog nibbles to her dolls?

I peeked around the corner into Victoria's room. She was sitting on the edge of her pink lacy comforter, eating the Doggy Do-Rights!

"Yummy treats!" she said, with a big smile, when she saw me. "Princess Daisy Do-Rights!"

Well, this certainly explained her recent bad breath.

"Gross!" I yelled. Victoria screamed when I took away her "treats," but for once Mom was on my side. She gave Victoria a lecture, gently of course, and then—I can still hardly believe it— she apologized to me.

"I shouldn't have assumed you were playing a practical joke, Tracy. I'll be more fair next time, I promise."

I nodded my head slowly, and looked at her with my best puppy dog eyes. How many chances would I get to milk an apology from Mom?

The next day, when Mom and Victoria put on matching dresses, I got out the special gifts I had made for them. Two matching necklaces, handcrafted by stringing Doggy Do-Rights on fishing line.

"You know, like those candy necklaces." I smiled. "Yummy treats! Eat up!"

Victoria lifted hers to her mouth, but Mom snatched it away. She glared at me, but then gave me a grudging smile.

"I know you wouldn't really have let her eat those," she said.

"Nope," I said. "Because I always know when to quit!" I smiled for real, and Mom gave me a little hug. Then, I dashed to my room before she could suggest that I wear a pink pastel cardigan or a lacy headband.

I know when to quit. But Mom? That's another story...matching outfits, anyone?

♦ ♦ ♦

Morning Girls

Emilie Ostrander

Callie has walked the walk all year, but could it be time for her friends to take a hike?

I'll admit it. It took weeks before I would even consider that Jamie and Morgan were being mean to me. I had excuses every time they excluded me. Like the time I rang Jamie's bell before school and no one answered. I started walking down Monroe Avenue, and I saw them a few blocks ahead. I yelled for them to wait up, but they didn't even turn around.

"Maybe they didn't hear me," I told Mom that night while we ate dinner. She just raised an eyebrow and took a steaming bite of casserole.

"Maybe," she said.

Okay, me and my excuses, but there was no way Jamie and Morgan didn't want to walk to school with me anymore. During third period the next day, Jamie slipped me a note saying it was nothing personal, but she and Morgan had been in the middle of a private conversation. It's not that they didn't want to wait for me, they just couldn't. They said they'd see me tomorrow morning and signed it "the morning girls."

"Say 'goodbye' to the morning girls," Mom said, making a funny face while she read the note. "Hmmph," she said when she finished reading.

"It's not like that," I told her. "Morgan was upset this morning and only wanted Jamie to know why."

"Morgan is *always* upset," Mom argued. "What is a 'morning girl' anyway?"

"My friends!" I said, snatching back the note. She just didn't understand.

She also didn't understand the time when my lunch disappeared. At Jamie's house before school, I realized I had left my English book at home. I had to go back and get it.

"I'll be right back. I have time." I told the morning girls. "Wait for me!"

"Okay," said Jamie.

"Whatever," said Morgan.

I raced back home, cutting through people's yards. I grabbed the book off my bed and was back in less than five minutes. Record time.

"Let's go," Morgan said, tossing me my backpack.

When I got to school, I unloaded my books into my locker. Then, I went to put my lunch on the shelf but it was missing. I emptied out my backpack and checked the front pouch. It was gone, and I knew I had packed it.

It wasn't in the fridge at home, either. That night, Mom said she knew who was to blame for the missing lunch. "They took your lunch," she said. "I didn't make stroganoff for the morning girls."

"Maybe I dropped it," I said. "I don't know why they'd take it."

"Callie," Mom said. "Get real."

"But why would they take it?"

"Think of it this way—what did you eat for lunch today?"

"I had to eat one of those boxed lunches the school gives out if you forget your lunch."

"Exactly," she said. "They just did it to give you a hard time." The school's boxed lunches were gross. The cafeteria supervisors made you take a boxed lunch if you didn't bring anything to eat. Eating the meal was like chomping on the cardboard box it came in. I ate half (the lunch, not the box) and threw the rest away. I was hungry all afternoon.

"Real friends don't do that," Mom said. She had a point, and I was out of excuses. Still, I told myself I just couldn't imagine the morning girls would take my lunch.

And then, there was the night we received four crank calls. I told myself that Jamie and Morgan would never make mean calls.

Mom and I were trying to watch TV and the phone kept ringing. During the first call, I could hear them laughing. I recognized their voices so I kept saying, "Jamie? Morgan? Is that you? Hello?"

But, they just laughed. Finally, Mom told me to hang up the phone.

The next call was clearly Morgan trying to impersonate a boy's voice.

"Is Callie there?" she asked.

"This is her," I said.

"Um...this is David. I wanted to let you know you have a really big forehead."

"Okay, thank you," I said and hung up. I didn't want Mom to know they had called again.

"Who was that?" she asked.

"No one, just a salesperson," I lied.

"Sales?" Mom asked and I nodded. She raised her eyebrow again. Mom let the answering machine pick up the third and fourth calls. One was them laughing again, the other one was Jamie and Morgan pretending to be my crush, Leo, telling me how I was the prettiest girl in math class and that he wanted to sit next to me. "If you like me," one of the morning girls said in a deep voice, "put a note in my locker."

"Nice friends," Mom said. "No more morning girls."

"What?!" No way. Who would I walk to school with?

"They're *not* your friends," she argued. "All they do is exclude you. They're mean to you, too."

"It's not like that," I whined.

"It *is*," she said. "I know it's hard to accept. You want people to like you. But, those two are *not* your friends."

"You don't know what they're really like," I said. "I don't want to talk about it. I'm going to bed."

"That's fine, Callie, but I'm giving you a ride to school tomorrow morning. No more morning girls."

I have to admit, it was a good thing Mom gave me a ride. If she hadn't, I probably would have caved and met the morning girls before school. But, I had devised a plan I wanted to put into action. I didn't want things to be like they were now. I wanted the morning girls to be like they used to be—no more crank calls or running ahead, shutting me out. I didn't know why they wanted to be mean to me. It just seemed like the harder I tried to be friends with them, the meaner they got. Now, I wondered, if I started acting like I didn't care, would the morning girls come crawling back? Is it even possible to exclude people when they've already excluded you?

My plan was to make the morning girls see what they were missing. Every time I did something to blow off the morning girls or acted like I didn't care, I'd earn a victory point. I figured by the time I reached ten points, Jamie and Morgan would start acting normal again. (I also told myself I could buy a new CD after ten points. A reward for not caving.)

I decided to try out my new plan that morning. Unlike most schools, my school makes us wait outside until the first bell. Rain or shine, we're standing on the blacktop waiting for the first bell. Everyone cliques-off and hangs in their own area. Normally, I'm with Jamie and Morgan, but that had to change. I couldn't just switch groups though—it was a sticky situation.

Mom, of course, dropped me off way before the morning bell.

"Sorry," she said when I groaned about having to wait five minutes extra on the blacktop. "It's a nice day," she offered. I gave her the look.

Since I was early, Jamie and Morgan weren't there yet and I had time to find a new distraction. I saw Rachel Levine standing with some of her friends, most of them from the volleyball team. Normally, I hate walking up to groups of people, but Jamie and Morgan could have been there any minute. I didn't want to be stranded.

"Hi," I said as I slid into their circle. Everyone said "hi" back, so that was no big deal. "Rachel," I asked. "Did you study for the Spanish quiz today?"

I swore she turned three different shades of green. "Uh, no," she gasped. "Is that today?"

I nodded somberly. "You need help?"

I was too busy reviewing Spanish vocab with Rachel to even notice when the morning girls arrived. I gave myself my first victory point. I even made Rachel laugh a couple of times with my impression of Señora Jones. I hoped the morning girls saw.

The next day in math class, Jamie tried to smile at me. I pretended not to see and scratched my arm instead. I gave myself another point.

When I got home that night, I told my mom about my plan.

"It seems like an awful lot of work," Mom said. She was checking my spelling homework and it was taking an eternity.

"It's worth it," I said.

"For what? You don't want to be friends with them again, right?"

"I don't know," I said.

Mom sighed. "Three wrong." She handed me back the paper with three red circles around my mistakes. "Rewrite the words you got wrong on a clean sheet."

That night, as I rewrote my answers, I thought about "the plan." It *was* worth it, I told myself. At least, I hoped it would be.

Having the plan helped me maneuver through a few situations that could have been unbearable. Morgan could be mean if she wanted to, and after school the next day, she was waiting by my locker.

"Where were you Tuesday morning?" she demanded. *The plan,* I told myself. *Think of the plan.* Normally, I would have caved and said I was sorry or whatever. I would have actually apologized for not letting them be mean to me. But, not this time. I had the plan.

"Where were you?" she asked again.

"Nowhere, *David*," I answered. I brushed past her and began unloading books from my backpack.

"*David?* What are you talking about?" She actually looked surprised. I just stood up and looked her in the eye while I slipped my arms through my backpack.

"Gotta go, Dave," I said coolly and walked away before she could say anything. Another point.

"Morgan was so mad," I told my mom that night. She was sewing my flapper costume for Rachel Levine's 1920's birthday bash. (Rachel got a 92% on the quiz, and I got an invite to her party. One point.)

"Let her be mad," Mom said, pulling thread through her fingers. "Besides, what do you care?"

"I don't know," I said sadly. "Morgan's really cool. She's pretty funny, and she has cool ideas."

"Like what—crank–calling her friends?" She adjusted the thimble on her finger.

"No, Morgan *can* be nice," I said. Mom didn't say anything. She just raised her eyebrow and gave me the look. But, it was true. Morgan *could* be pretty nice. But, she could also be really vicious. So, I knew what to expect the next day during third period when Jamie handed me a note. "It's from Morgan," she said blankly.

"Um, no thanks," I said.

"*Excuse me?*"

"No thanks," I repeated. "Return to sender."

Jamie just stood there.

I couldn't resist. "Besides, I have a lot of notes to write," I said sarcastically. "I'm supposed to write one to Leo first."

Jamie totally got it. She stood there looking for something good to say. "Morgan's going to be mad," she finally said.

"Let her," I answered coolly. I turned and faced forward, letting her know I was finished talking. I gave myself a point.

So, now I was at the halfway mark. But things weren't working out the way I had planned. Excluding the morning girls didn't make them miss me or think about how mean they had been to me. It just made them mad at me.

I heard from Kelly—the girl with the locker next to mine—that Morgan had been looking for me after school on Friday afternoon. I wasn't there. I was at my first ever yearbook meeting. (One point.)

I guess Morgan hoped to confront me Monday morning, but I was too busy trying out for the speech team. (Another point.) Morgan put a note in my locker. Probably 'cause she couldn't track me down.

I didn't even read the note. I just passed it off to Jamie during third period. "Didn't read it," I said. "I don't have time for Morgan's attitude." (One point.)

Jamie got a sour look on her face. "You better watch out," she said. She looked so little in her desk, I didn't even feel afraid of her anymore.

"For what?"

She thought for a moment. "You're going to make Morgan mad."

"Who cares?" I asked. I walked away before she could answer.

The next day, I walked to school alone for the first time. It wasn't as big of a deal as I thought it would be. When I got to the blacktop, I felt a knot in my stomach, but then I saw two girls from yearbook, Abbey and Brooke. Abbey's the funniest person I've ever met, and Brooke's super-sweet.

We were sitting against the brick wall when I saw the morning girls standing by the tetherball pole. *Weird*, I thought. *That's not their normal spot.* It seems like the further I pulled away from the morning girls, the closer they got. It was like they were mad at me for not letting them pick on me anymore.

I was beginning to see the bad side of the morning girls. Jamie was weak and Morgan just liked to argue with people. I don't think she's happy unless she can argue. I could hear her saying loudly to Jamie, "ABC, Abbey, Brooke, and Callie. How cute. Callie's an ABC now." Jamie just sneered.

Abbey and Brooke ignored the morning girls, but I was watching them closely. That's when I saw the tetherball swing wildly around the pole and whack Morgan in the back of the head. She started freaking out really hard. Yelling at the boys playing tetherball and threatening to tell.

We silently watched Morgan's meltdown. I have to admit, I was slightly enjoying the tetherball whack.

"What did she expect when she's standing in front of the tetherball pole?" asked Brooke, seeming slightly bored with Morgan's tantrum.

"I don't know. I guess she's just a mean baby," answered Abbey.

"Yeah," we all chorused together.

For the first time in a long time, I realized I really didn't want to be a morning girl. In fact, I was *glad* I wasn't a morning girl.

"Hey," said Brooke. "Didn't you used to hang out with Jamie and Morgan?" The way she asked, it wasn't like she was judging me. She was just asking.

"Yeah, I used to," I said.

"And now?"

I thought for a moment. "Not anymore," I said with a smile.

Graduation

Patricia Bridgman

Sarah graduates to a new understanding of what's really important in life: Friendship. Compassion. And a good electric razor.

SUNDAY

I'm looking in the mirror and cutting off my hair with scissors. I had just finally gotten my bangs to grow out, too. This is worse than I expected.

Soon, the sink is full of hair. It's *my* hair, but it looks creepy, like it's somebody else's. There are raggedy clumps sticking out all over my head. I look like a cartoon. I cut the clumps close to my scalp. I can hardly see what I'm doing, I'm crying so hard. Dad's shaving cream. Mom's razor.

Ow! Eleven years old, and I've cut myself shaving. I don't even shave my legs yet, and here I am shaving my head. I stick toilet paper on the cut to stop the bleeding. Very attractive.

Think my family notices my head when I wear a baseball cap to the dinner table? Oh, they notice.

"Lose the hat, Sarah, please," Dad says. He asked for it. I lose the hat. Everybody stares at my head. Mom's mouth moves, but no words come out.

Dad pats her shoulder. My brother Ben laughs 'til milk comes out of his nose.

"I got bubble gum in it, all right?" I say. That's all the explaining I feel like doing. If I'd asked permission beforehand, they'd have said no. So I didn't. Case closed.

MONDAY

Joke: What should a bald girl wear to school? Mohair. Ha. Ha.

Like it matters what I wear. Nobody's gonna be looking at my clothes. This all just feels totally weird.

I breeze through the kitchen before anybody can say anything. "I'll have a granola bar on the bus," I say, and I'm out the door.

The kids on the school bus are out of control, as usual. Then I get on. Everybody freezes. The yelling stops. Spitballs hang in mid-air. If I could disappear, I would.

Kathy always saves me a seat. When she sees me, she grabs her own hair, which is straight and blonde and everybody's jealous of. Her jaw drops.

"Don't look at me like that," I say.

"Don't look at *me* like that," she says.

When we get to class, a few of the guys giggle and point at yours truly. Everyone else has that deer-in-the-headlights look.

Could you all puleeez look at something else, I think to myself.

Ms. Washington is looking, too. She smiles. "This is for Wednesday, I assume?" she asks me. And with that, we begin our second-to-last day at Benton Elementary.

After school, Kathy gets off the bus at my stop. "Okay, I'm in," she says. "But you have to do it for me. I can't."

Kathy and I both cry as her hair hits the bathroom floor. It is so beautiful. *Was* so beautiful. I've learned my lesson about ladies' so-called safety razors. I use Dad's electric instead. Kathy and I look at her reflection in the mirror.

Kathy's a sissy sometimes, but she's brave when it counts. "I like it," she says.

"Yay!" I say.

This is why Kathy is my best friend in the world.

TUESDAY

I have to use Dad's electric shaver while I'm getting ready for school. I've got whiskers on my head. Not many girls can pull off a look like this.

The bus is quiet again today. The sight of Kathy bald has everybody stupefied.

Half the kids are already in their desks when Kathy and I walk into Ms. Washington's room. Now it's *our* turn to be stupefied. There are Freddie, Paula "Popcorn" Phillips, Heather, Emma, and Myles. Bald,

bald, bald, bald, and bald. Popcorn points at Kathy and says, "Girrrl!" in that way she has. Popcorn and Kathy high-five. We all high-five.

I never thought Heather and Emma liked Kathy and me. They sort of run with another crowd. Guess I was wrong about them. You can't judge a book by its cover, as the saying goes.

WEDNESDAY

Today, we graduate from sixth grade. I'm almost used to being bald, so I hardly feel bad when I see myself in the mirror in my white graduation dress.

Mom and I picked it out a couple weeks ago. She cried when I tried it on—said I looked like a bride. Hope she doesn't cry when she sees me in it today.

She doesn't cry, but she does hug me for about ten minutes, no lie.

We're running late. My jerk of a brother won't put on a tie like Dad wants him to. Ben points out that Mom and Dad don't make me wear hair if I don't want to.

"That's different," Dad says.

When we get to the auditorium, I hurry into my chair on stage, next to Kathy.

Know what a double take is? Where you look at something, look away, and then look back real fast? Well, that's just what I do now. Everyone in my entire class is bald.

Kathy and I look around at all the other bald kids. Gianna has glued a flower above her left ear. Edgar's forehead says, "This End Up" in magic marker. Walt is wearing these hilarious eyeballs on springs taped to his scalp.

Principal Wright walks onto the stage. He's bald but then again, he's always been bald. He welcomes the audience and talks about the "brave new world" we're headed for.

By this, he means Kennedy Middle School. He says he's never been prouder of any other graduating class, ever. Then, he brings out our teacher, Ms. Washington.

She's bald.

Suddenly, everybody's on their feet, cheering and clapping. The place goes wild.

"Thank you," she yells, over the commotion. "And please welcome back...Joannie Ebert!"

Joannie walks onstage. She is skinnier and taller than I remember. Oh, yeah, she's bald, too. But we expected her to be bald. She turns to all of us and says through tears, "I love you guys!"

Joannie got cancer at the end of fifth grade last year. The medicine made her hair fall out and she had to stay away from school for almost this whole year so she wouldn't catch our germs. But she's okay now. If she can stay okay for five years, she'll be fine.

Last week, Ms. Washington told us that Joannie would be coming back for graduation. She asked us to put ourselves in Joannie's shoes and make her feel at home.

Now that Joannie's had the last of her treatments, she'll be going on to Kennedy with us in the fall. I wonder if our hair will grow back by then.

The Crush Crisis

Diana Koulechova, age 11

Chris is Diana's first crush. Will "love" blossom...
or will she be the one crushed?

"Everyone on stage!" a voice rang out in Markham Middle School's auditorium. Kids ran all around the room. An old man with a white beard was looking at them. He was ready to speak. The old man eyed the students, and they eyed him.

"Okay, um," he started, but his words were lost in all the noise the students were making. "Quiet!" he shouted, and a dead silence hit the room. He gave a speech about the drama class not being a class, him not being a teacher, and the children not being students. "You are actors, and I am a director," he said.

Diana wasn't really listening. She was preoccupied. When drama class ended, everyone left the auditorium like a herd of wild horses. "Bye, Jade!" Diana shouted to the girl with brown eyes and dark pony-tailed hair.

"See ya!" Jade shouted back.

They got into their parents' cars.

Diana's mom asked, "So, are you doing the same play as last year?"

"Yeah," Diana said. Usually, she was more excited after drama. Not today.

"If you don't want to talk about it, we don't have to. Just tell me what's wrong."

"Just confused, I guess."

"About what?"

"I want to be a seventh-grader. I don't want to be younger than all my friends."

Diana's mom just shook her head—she couldn't help her there—and they rode home in silence.

♦ ♦ ♦

JANUARY 25

Dear Diary,

Today, I found another reason for wanting to be a seventh-grader. It all started at recess when I was walking by the seventh-grade classrooms. I saw a guy. Not just any guy. He's tall and gorgeous. So now, I officially have a crush. There wouldn't be a problem with that except for the fact that the guy doesn't know I exist. I looked him up in the yearbook. Now I know his name. It's Chris Lemmend.

◆ ◆ ◆

Next time Diana went to drama class, she brought along her yearbook. She knew she had to show someone. And that someone had to be Jade. No one else would understand.

"Jade, can we talk?" Diana asked Jade.

"Sure. What about?"

Diana didn't know how to begin. "So, how are things going between you and…"

"Fine…except."

"Except what?"

"I know that's not what you want to talk about."

"You're right. I want to talk about…," Diana swallowed a lump in her throat, "my crush."

"You have a crush?! Congratulations! Who is he?"

"Chris Lemmend. Seventh–grader. But he doesn't even know I exist. What did you do when…"

"When I had my crush? Nothing."

"*Nothing?*"

"I was too embarrassed to do anything. Then one day, my friends asked me if I knew he liked me."

"But none of my friends know Chris."

"Hmmm. Maybe you should just wait."

"Okay I'll try."

"Good luck, Diana."

♦ ♦ ♦

The next day, Diana saw him again, walking with a friend of his. But luckily, Chris's friend's locker was right next to hers! The "in" she needed! So, she managed to have a little conversation with Chris's friend next time they were both at their lockers.

"Hey," Diana said when she saw him.

"Are you a new kid?" Chris's friend asked.

"No. I've gone to Markham since last year."

"Really? Whose class are you in?"

"Mrs. Stein's," Diana answered.

"Mrs. Stein is a sixth-grade teacher."

"I know. *I'm* a sixth-grader."

"Oh, great. A puny little sixth-grader."

"I'm a sixth-grader, but I'm *not* puny."

"Yeah, right. Go play with your dolls."

Diana was so sad. She couldn't just shout insults back at him. After all, he was a friend of Chris's. But she couldn't just take insults from him either. *I wonder what Jade would do,* Diana thought as she walked sadly toward her classroom.

Later, Diana realized the day had not been a total loss. She *had* talked with Chris's friend. Unfortunately, the impression she left was not a very good one—not that *he* had left a good impression either, but still....

I wish I were a seventh-grader, Diana thought to herself. *Then, maybe Chris and I would be friends. But I don't have a chance. He would just think I'm babyish.* Diana grabbed a piece of paper and a pencil. This is what she wrote:

1. SHOW HIM I'M NOT A BABY.

I'll keep a list of ideas on how to become Chris's friend, she thought. *One of them is bound to work.* That night Diana lay in her bed peacefully. She wasn't dreading the day ahead anymore.

"Take out English, page 98," Mrs. Stein said. The students did as they were told. "We're going to the computer lab now. And then to the library."

"But what about P.E.?" someone asked.

"No P.E. because of computer lab," Mrs. Stein replied.

"Yes!" the kids shouted. None of them could stand the P.E. instructor. While walking to computer lab, Diana got another idea, inspired by her friend Madison, who was chatting about her older brother's friends. "They used to think I was a goof and wouldn't even talk to me. That is, until they saw me Rollerblade."

"And that helped?" Diana asked.

"Sure," Madison said. Then she changed her voice to imitate her brother's friends, "You know, she's all right for a sixth-grader." When she got to the library, Diana added to her list:

2. IMPRESS HIM BY DOING SOMETHING COOL.

♦ ♦ ♦

Diana was late for drama class and hurried toward the auditorium. Jade came running down the hallway.

"Hi! Any luck?" Jade asked.

"No. None. But I did *get* an idea that just might help me solve my crush problem."

"Really? What?"

Diana took her list from her pocket.

"*Show him I'm not a baby. Impress him by doing something cool,*" Jade read out loud. "What is this?"

"I figure if I write down a bunch of ideas, one of them is sure to work."

Then, their friend Spencer walked up.

"Hey, what are you guys talking about?" Spencer asked. Jade gave Diana a 'Can I tell him?' look. Diana shook her head no. Jade nodded.

"Nothing, really. Just talking about when I had my crush," Jade told him.

"Really? I guess you're over it now."

"Actually, the guy likes me, too."

"You're lucky. When I had my crush, I liked a girl in sixth grade, and I was in fifth. She didn't know I existed."

"What did you do?" Diana asked. The situation sounded mighty familiar to her.

"I met her and found out she wasn't really very nice," Spencer said.

Diana's list looked like this that night:

1. SHOW HIM I'M NOT A BABY.

2. IMPRESS HIM BY DOING SOMETHING COOL.

3. MEET HIM.

4. DECIDE IF HE'S NICE, ONCE I GET TO KNOW HIM.

The list was getting longer, but Diana still had no solution to her problem. It now controlled her life. It was all she ever thought about.

♦ ♦ ♦

The next day at school, Diana deliberately walked past the seventh-grade rooms, hoping to catch a glimpse of Chris Lemmend. As she looked around for him, she noticed a girl crying in the corner.

Diana walked up to her. She wasn't very big. Blond curls hung forward and covered the girl's face, which was buried in her blue jumper. Diana didn't know what to think.

"Are you okay?" she asked the girl.

The girl looked up. "Who are you?" she asked. Her face was quite pretty, even though it was all stained with tears. Her big blue eyes were red from all the crying.

"I'm Diana. What's your name?"

"I'm Amy," the girl answered.

"Why are you crying?" Diana asked.

"Well, this boy stole my new notebook. And he poured red juice on my new shirt. My mom's going to kill me."

Diana was appalled. "What boy?"

"His name is Chris. His last name begins with L or something like that. I think it's Lemon."

"Oh, my gosh!" Diana's eyes were wide. *Could Chris do that? Nah.* Diana shook her head. Couldn't be. Maybe Amy did something mean to Chris first. After all, she didn't know Amy. Diana decided to give her crush the benefit of the doubt until she was able to meet him face to face. But the next day, she found out the truth about Chris.

She was walking along when she saw a first-grader crying just outside the girls' bathroom. She walked up to her. If the little girl's black hair hadn't been pulled back in a braid, Diana wouldn't have seen how very red her eyes were from crying. She saw a rip in the red jumper the girl was wearing, and black stains on the sleeves of her white turtleneck.

"What's the matter?" Diana asked the little girl. "What's your name?"

"Sally," the little girl answered. "And this seventh-grade boy, Chris, was teasing me for being a first-grader, and then he tripped me. When I fell, I ripped my jumper and ruined my shirt."

"Sheesh," Diana said. "Are you okay?"

"Yeah, I'm going back to class now."

The little girl left, and Diana went inside the bathroom to think. *To be mean to someone your own age is bad, but to bully someone a lot younger is really awful*, she thought to herself. *I don't even care if I ever meet him now. Actually, I'd rather not.*

Diana pulled out her notebook. She turned to the page that had her list and she ripped it out of her notebook. She wadded up the paper and tossed it in the trash can. The Chris crisis was history... but, hey, who's *that* cutie coming down the hall?

Sergeant Beckles

Alison Embrey

When dads have to fight, daughters have to deal.
See how one girl comes to terms with having to
say "goodbye" to her father as he goes off to war.

Rebecca Rivers looked down, disappointed as the big, ugly lunch lady dumped a nasty glob of brown goo onto her green lunch tray. *Aw, gross*, she thought to herself as she tried to figure out what she would be eating today, though she would never say that out loud to The Beastwoman, as the mean lunch server was secretly dubbed by the students.

As Rebecca looked up, she saw The Beastwoman angrily eyeing her from behind the tips of her black hairnet.

"Somethin' wrong with your stew?" she asked, raising her ladle up in the air as if she were about to attack.

"No, ma'am. Looks delicious," Rebecca answered convincingly. She knew better than to give any other answer to The Beastwoman— or suffer the consequences.

Eager to get away from The Beastwoman's glare, Rebecca quickly grabbed an apple and some chocolate milk, swiped her lunch card, and turned to find her table. Scanning the cafeteria for her usual lunch crowd, Rebecca smiled as she spotted Jessica across the room. Jess had saved her a spot at the lunch table, as usual.

"Hey, Beck, brown mush again today?" Jessica asked mockingly. She (Jessica) had her usual lunch menu laid out in front of her—sushi, carrots, and a bottle of Evian water. Her outfit today was especially Jessica: pink sweater and jeans, plus matching pink shoes, pink hat, pink purse, and even a little furry pink cell phone holder.

Jess was the only twelve-year-old Rebecca knew who was allowed to have a cell phone. Rebecca's dad thought it was insane to "give a device like that to a child." It wasn't surprising though, considering Jessica's weekly allowance was more money than Rebecca had ever seen in her life.

"Very funny, dork. I'll stick with the apple and milk. Does a body good," Rebecca said, wiping off her apple with a napkin.

"So are you excited about your trip this weekend?" Jess asked, bored with the food discussion and ready to move on to the next topic. The two girls had been friends since the day Rebecca moved to town, two years ago. Jessica had been assigned to show her around school her first day, giving her the grand tour and introducing her to all the teachers. By the time they had seen the gym, cafeteria, library, computer lab, and principal's office, the two had already decided they were going to be best friends for life. They had been lowly fourth-graders then, and now, as sixth-graders, they were pretty much inseparable.

"I'm so, so, *so* excited!! Can you believe it? I wish Mom didn't have to work, so she could go, too, but Dad and I have never taken a trip before, just the two of us. He's planned out the whole thing, just for us. We're gonna see a baseball game on Saturday, and pig out on Cracker Jacks and nachos, then camp out in the woods with a bonfire and marshmallows that night, and on Sunday, we're going to this aquarium that's supposed to have the biggest shark tank you've ever seen and..."

"Rebecca! Enough already. You're excited—I get it. Calm down, please," Jess said, rolling her eyes. But Rebecca didn't care. She was excited about this weekend. So excited she could hardly stand sitting in class that morning. She just dazed off into her own world, doodling in her notebook about all the things she still had to pack when she got home from school. *Toothbrush. Bug spray. Baseball hat. Clean socks. Marshmallows.* There was so much to do! Her dad was picking her up an hour early from school so they could run home, gather up all their stuff, and get out on the road. She only had to wait halfway through her science lesson before he'd be here, but it still seemed so far away.

"I know, I know. I'm sorry. This is just going to be the best trip. I can't wait to get out of here!" Rebecca said, taking a bite of her apple.

"Hey, when you are out with the bears and the bugs this weekend, maybe you can talk to your dad about that stupid nickname he has for you. Doesn't he know it's embarrassing?" Jess asked, biting into a crunchy carrot.

"Yeah...it's totally lame. It's just something he's called me since I was a little girl," Rebecca answered, hoping Jess couldn't see through her lie.

Rebecca actually *loved* that her dad called her "Beckles." It was her special name, and every time her dad called her that, it was always followed by a hug or kiss. Even when he was all dressed up in his military clothes, he would say, "Hey, Beckles, how about a hug for your old man?" and sweep her up off her feet in a big cuddle. Her dad was the best soldier she knew, and when she was little, she loved when he let her put on his Army clothes. She'd march around the house in his big black boots with the sleeves hanging down to her ankles, tripping over herself the whole time. Her dad even made her an Army-green T-shirt that read "Sergeant Beckles" on the front. She slept in that shirt every night for a year until it was so holey, her mom made her throw it away.

"Well, I have to run to the library to return a book that's way overdue. I'll see you after school, right?" Jess asked, gathering up her leftover sushi crumbs and sticking her Evian in her pink purse for later.

"Nope. Leaving early, remember?" Rebecca couldn't help but smile at the thought.

Jess twisted her face in a weird frown. "Oh, yeah. Too bad. I'll have to walk home by myself. Ughhhh!" She was full-out whining now. She had a tendency to do that when she didn't get her way.

"Yep, sorry, Jess. I'm outta here."

◆ ◆ ◆

An hour later, Rebecca eagerly eyed the clock, waiting for the minute hand to creep to 2 p.m. and hear her name called to the office for checkout over the loudspeaker. When the clock did indeed, finally, hit 2:00, Rebecca was disappointed when the familiar buzz from the office didn't come. *How strange,* she thought. Her dad was never late. At 2:06, she was very antsy. At 2:15, she began tapping on her desk. At 2:27, she felt like her head was about to burst with curiosity— *where was he?*

At 2:42, Rebecca couldn't take it anymore. She raised her hand.

Mrs. Crandell stopped in the middle of her lesson on rainforests, and, for the first time, noticed Rebecca wriggling about in her seat.

"Rebecca, do you have to go to the bathroom?" she asked. The entire class broke out in stifled giggles. Rebecca didn't care.

"No, ma'am. But my dad was supposed to pick me up at 2:00 so we could leave for our trip, but he's not here yet. Can I go to the office to call home and see what's taking him so long?"

Mrs. Crandell opened up her mouth to speak but was interrupted by the buzz of the loudspeaker. Rebecca eagerly jumped out of her seat and grabbed her backpack in one swift motion. Finally!

"Mrs. Crandell, Rebecca Rivers' mother is here to check her out," rang the voice from the office.

Mother? Rebecca was confused. Her *father* was supposed to pick her up. Her mother wasn't supposed to get off work for a few more hours. Maybe the office lady made a mistake…

"Go ahead, Rebecca. We'll see you on Monday. Have a nice weekend, dear," Mrs. Crandell said.

Rebecca darted out of the room, anxious to get home and finish packing. When she got to the front office, she asked, "What are you doing here, Mom?"

"Well, nice to see you too, sweetie," she said. "Your father, he…" Her mother grabbed Rebecca's two hands and pulled her in close to her. Rebecca knew something was wrong. Her mom had a funny look on her face. "You know how Dad's been telling you about all the problems that are going on right now in countries all over the world, right? Well, the problems don't seem to be getting any better."

Rebecca's father always told her about how some countries don't have a government system like America does, with a president and Congress and all that. Some countries are run by leaders who don't let their citizens make any decisions, and it's sad for the people because they can't do anything to stop it. Some leaders are even a threat to other countries.

But Rebecca didn't see what any of this had to do with the fact that her father wasn't here to pick her up like he was supposed to. "Our government wants to do everything it can to make sure

Americans are safe," Rebecca's mother continued. "You know what Dad does for a living, sweetie, right?"

Rebecca thought it was an odd question. "He's in the Army, Mom. Of course I know that."

"And what does the Army do?"

"Well, Dad says the Army protects the country…" Rebecca looked up at her mother, finally realizing. "Mom, does Dad have to go away?"

Her mother looked down at her feet for a quick second, and when she looked back up at Rebecca, her eyes were glazed over in tears. "Yes, honey," she said, her voice cracking slightly. "Dad has to leave tomorrow to fight in the Middle East."

Rebecca stared at her mother in disbelief. Was this really happening? War was something she only learned about in school, not something that was real. She didn't know what to think. She didn't care about leaving school early anymore. She didn't care about missing her weekend trip. The only thing on Rebecca's mind was her father. Was he really leaving for war? And tomorrow? "How long will he have to be gone?" Rebecca asked, trying not to cry.

"I don't know," her mother answered, trying to hold back her own tears. "I just don't know."

♦ ♦ ♦

Early the next morning, before the sun was even up, Rebecca awoke to her mother gently shaking her. Rebecca groggily opened her eyes, though she didn't want to wake up at all. As soon as she got up out of bed and went downstairs, she knew what was waiting for her. Her father would be fully dressed in his camouflage clothes, waiting patiently to say "goodbye" before…before going to fight overseas.

Reluctantly, Rebecca dragged herself out of bed and got her robe and slippers on. "Come on, sweetie. Dad is waiting outside." Sure enough, when they got out to the driveway, her father was standing in uniform by an Army-looking car Rebecca had never seen before.

As she walked toward him, her father made the best smile he could muster. But Rebecca could tell he was doing everything he could not to cry. She bit her lip and clenched her fists tightly, as she joined him at the base of the driveway. She was, very suddenly, absolutely terrified. She didn't know what she was scared of, but she was so scared, she was actually shaking.

Rebecca's father rested both his hands on her shoulders and looked her right in the eye, still with a smile on his face. "Well, Sergeant Beckles. It's time for me to get this show on the road."

Rebecca, unable to bear the thought of her father actually letting go of her, threw her arms around his waist and squeezed as tight as she could. She thought the tighter she squeezed, the longer he would stay. She wanted him to never go away.

"But I don't want you to go, Dad. I don't want you to go at all," she screamed, unable to hold back her tears.

"Look at me, Rebecca," he said, his eyes now just as wet with tears as hers. "I am very, very proud of you. You are the best daughter any dad could ever have wished for in a million years. You always remember that, no matter what. I love you, sweetheart."

"I love you, too, Dad. I love you, too."

♦ ♦ ♦

Over the next several months, Rebecca missed her father terribly. She watched all the TV newscasts with her mother, hoping to catch a glimpse of her father in one of the shots of soldiers fighting the war. She tried to learn as much as she could about what the Americans were trying to do, why they were trying to bring down a foreign country's leader, and, most important, when her dad and the rest of the soldiers might be able to come back home.

All the kids in her school wrote cards and letters, made care packages, and drew pictures to send to Rebecca's father and other soldiers. She knew her dad would appreciate all that attention, even from the stupid boys who teased her sometimes. Mrs. Crandell wanted the class to understand what the war was about, and made it a point for her students to send cards and packages to the American soldiers in the Middle East every week.

Every time the phone rang at home, Rebecca darted to pick up the receiver, always disappointed when it was only a relative or family friend checking in to make sure she and her mother were okay. She ran home from school every day, to check the mailbox and her e-mail for letters. Writing had become the only way she could communicate with her father.

She wrote him every day, telling him what had happened at school, what grades she got on her tests, or what cool thing she had learned in history. She told him what her mom was doing, what movies she and Jessica had seen, and how long her hair had gotten. She always drew a great big red-white-and-blue flag somewhere on the page, just to make sure her dad knew just how proud she was of him. She wanted, more than anything, for her dad to come home. To hug her until she couldn't breathe.

His letters didn't come as often as hers were sent off, but Rebecca understood how busy he was. He wrote whenever he could, and always sent a separate letter for her mom. Rebecca would always stare at her letter for several minutes before actually opening it. Sometimes getting a new letter made her sad because it meant her dad wasn't coming home yet, that he still had to visit her through words on a page. But mostly, those letters were magical. They were the link that kept her in touch with her dad, the greatest soldier in the world.

♦ ♦ ♦

Dear Dad,

I miss you. I put a picture of you on my desk at school. Some of the stupid boys in my class laughed at me, but I don't care. I think about you a lot. My friends ask about you a lot, too, because they know I'm worried. But I know you'll be fine. You always find a way to make the best of a bad situation. Let me know if you need anything, okay? I have hugs and kisses tucked in my back pocket for the day I get to see you again. I can't wait until you come home.

Love you, Beckles

Dear Sergeant Beckles,

I miss you, too, sweetie. It's hard being over here by myself, without being able to tuck you in at night, or kiss you in the morning. But every day that goes by is just one day closer to the day I get to come home and see you. I have a picture of you and your mother hanging over my bed here. Your beautiful, smiling faces are the first thing I see in the morning, and the last thing I see before going to sleep at night.

Take care of your mama for me. And tell your friend Jessica not to stay on that ridiculous cell phone all night long! I love you very, very much. I can't wait to see you. We'll stretch that weekend trip into a two-week vacation when I get back, okay? Just you and me, kiddo.

Love, Dad

♦ ♦ ♦

The Blizzard

Kristen Weber

A major blizzard has been predicted all week,
but 14-year old Haley Peters is too focused
on her movie plans with her crush, Jake, to notice.
Until the storm of the century strikes...

I am sitting in the bedroom I share with my two sisters, putting the finishing touches on a paper for my English class. It's due tomorrow, and I've been putting it off all week. The weather forecaster had been predicting a major snow since Monday, so I was holding out hope for a day off. Even though I live in Vermont, my school closes if there is so much as a flake. As I cross the final "t," my five-year-old sister, Peggy, runs in.

"Haley," she says, "I'm hungry."

"What would you like?" I ask.

Peggy wrinkles her forehead in thought. Finally she says, "Chocolate cake."

"Chocolate cake? I don't think we have any." I stand up and take Peggy's hand. "Let's go check."

Peggy and I walk into the kitchen. The cottage we live in with our mom and other sister, Lauren, who's 10, is so tiny that it isn't much of a walk. When we get into the kitchen, we find Lauren perched on a chair, her eyes glued to the tiny TV Mom picked up at a garage sale.

"What are you watching?" I ask Lauren, as I look through the cabinets for anything even remotely resembling chocolate cake.

Lauren tears her eyes away from the screen. *"Hollywood Squares."*

I groan. Lauren is a game show fanatic. She never misses any game show that airs between the hours of 3:00 and 5:00. Those are the hours we're home alone after school while Mom is at work. I know Mom would never approve if she knew the extent of Lauren's game show addiction, but it's just easier to let her watch than to argue with her.

Lauren brushes her blonde hair away from her face and turns back to the TV. I have the same color hair, and so do Mom and Peggy. We all have the same blue eyes and the same nose. I'm the only one with freckles.

"Haley? Chocolate cake?"

"Sorry, Peg." I say, opening the refrigerator and quickly closing it. There isn't much to choose from. Hopefully, Mom will stop at the grocery store on her way home from the law office where she works as a paralegal. "There's bread or some fruit."

"Yuck!" Peggy sticks out her tongue. "Will Mom bring pizza home?"

"Maybe." Just as the words are out of my mouth, the phone rings. I grab it. "Hello?"

"Haley, it's Mom. How's everything going?"

"Fine." I say. "Can you get pizza on the way home?" My mom is sometimes too tired to make dinner after work, so she just picks up pizza or I make us all one of the two dishes I'm good at—macaroni and cheese with hot dogs or grilled cheese sandwiches.

"I'm not sure what time I'm going to be home. I have to finish this case report. I tried to call Mrs. Duncan to see if she could come by, but she isn't home."

Mrs. Duncan is our next-door neighbor who watches us when Mom gets stuck at work. She smells like cats and doesn't let us watch TV for more than a few minutes. But, at the moment, that's the least of my worries. I'm planning to go out tonight.

"Mom!" I exclaim. "I have plans to go to the movies. With Jake!"

"Ooh, Jake." Mom's voice takes on a teasing quality I don't appreciate. "I'm sorry, honey, but you'll have to cancel. Plus, it's supposed to snow pretty hard tonight. I'm sure his parents won't let him go either."

Sigh. I'm sure Mom is just saying it might dump snow to make me feel better. Lately, I haven't been able to go to a lot of places Jake invites me. Last week, after I broke plans with him for Alicia Hickman's party, he complained that I'm always babysitting my sisters or doing something with my family. I know it's true, but I don't have a whole lot of choice in the matter. I have to help Mom. Since she and my dad split, it's just us four girls.

"OK, Mom. Don't worry. We'll be fine."

"You're the best!" I can hear the relief in Mom's voice. "Give Lauren and Peggy a hug from me. Now, you know the rules. Make sure the doors are locked, and don't open them for anyone! I'll call you when I'm about to leave."

I hang up with Mom and then wait for the dial tone. A rock has settled into my stomach. The same rock that always seems to be there whenever I think of Jake. I dial his number.

"Hello?" It's Jake's voice.

"Hey Jake. It's Haley."

"Hey. What's up? Looking forward to *Revenge of the Ant Women*?"

"Actually, I can't make it. I have to watch my sisters tonight. My mom's stuck at work."

"So you're canceling again?"

"Sorry, I have to help out."

After more silence than I'm comfortable with, Jake gets out, "Sure, sure—I understand," in a not-very understanding voice.

Before I can even think of something to salvage the situation, Peggy is clinging to my legs and I hang up.

"Haley? Where's Mom?"

"Mom is working late, Peg. She'll call us when she's on her way home."

"Haley, look!" Peggy points to the window.

Guess Mom and the weather people weren't totally making this storm up. All of a sudden, it's snowing—a lot. It looks like a big, white, fluffy blanket covering our window.

"Snow? *Finally!*" Lauren leaps up and speeds toward the window. I've never seen her move so fast during *Hollywood Squares*. "Wow!"

Peggy and Lauren are silent for a few minutes. Then, they both speak at once.

"Can we play in it? Can we build a snowman?"

I look down at my sisters. "Mom says we should stay inside. We should wait until she gets home."

"But she won't be home for hours." Lauren whines. "The snow will be gone!"

While I doubt this snow is going anywhere, I look down at their eager faces and give in. We've been waiting for the snow all week, and finally it's here. "Okay, put on your jackets."

My sisters cheer and run out of the kitchen.

◆ ◆ ◆

"Look at me, Haley! I'm a snow snake." Peggy wiggles on the snow-covered ground and slithers toward me.

I laugh, but I'm starting to feel nervous. The snow is falling really quickly. At first, it was the fluffy kind that melts when you catch it on your tongue, but now it's more like tiny pebbles. We're only a few yards from our house, but it's getting harder to see the door through the falling snow.

"Haley? I'm cold." Lauren appears in front of me almost out of nowhere.

"Okay, let's go inside." I pull Peggy to her feet and grab Lauren's hand. Together, we practically skate to our front door.

"Watch the steps," I tell them. Our previously harmless front stoop now looks like a dangerous ice slide. Peggy giggles as I push her through the front door, but I don't find anything funny when it's my turn to boost myself over the ice.

Once we're inside, I help my sisters out of their wet, snowy clothes. Then Lauren sits down to watch TV, and Peggy turns to me eagerly. "*Now* is it time for chocolate cake?"

I shake my head. "Maybe later."

The phone rings just as Peggy sits down to play with her dolls. I grab it. "Hello?"

It's Mom. "Hi, Haley. Listen, I have bad news. I can't get home tonight. It's awful out, and there's an accident on Route 110. The whole road is closed. I've tried to call Mrs. Duncan again, but she still isn't home. You're going to have to be in charge."

My heart almost stops at those words. I babysit my sisters all the time but usually only after school. If Mom is going to be more than a few hours late, Mrs. Duncan always comes over. But I can tell from Mom's voice that there isn't much choice. "Don't worry, Mom. I can handle things here."

" Okay, Haley. Make sure Peg and Lauren are both in bed on time, and don't stay up too late yourself. Can you scrounge up something for dinner?"

I know there's almost nothing in the fridge, but I don't want to add to Mom's worries. So I just say, "Sure. We'll be fine."

"Okay. Let me talk to Peggy and Lauren. I want to say goodnight to them."

I give the phone to Peggy, and tell Lauren she should talk to Mom when Peg is finished. Peggy will probably cry briefly when Mom tells her she isn't coming home, but she usually can be easily distracted. Lauren should be happy because she'll get away with a few more hours of watching TV.

I scrounge through the kitchen cabinets and all I can find to eat is a box of Sugar Snaps cereal. I make us each a bowl, that we quickly scarf down. Then, I flip on the light by a reading chair, pick up a magazine, and try to take a friendship quiz, but I just keep thinking of Jake.

He and I became friends when we were assigned to be lab partners in bio. So far, we've been to three school dances together, seen four movies, and had dinner at his house once.

I haven't been daydreaming for more than 10 minutes when I hear an angry shout from the kitchen. "Hey!" cries Lauren. "What happened to *Jeopardy*?"

I get up and hurry into the kitchen. Lauren is staring at a TV filled with gray and white snow. "And right before Final Jeopardy!"

"The cable must have gone out," I tell Lauren. No sooner are the words out of my mouth when we plummet into darkness.

Peggy cries, "Mommy!"

I scoop her off the floor and give her a hug. "Shhh, it's OK. The power just went out."

The house is so dark, I can hardly see anything in front of me. Light isn't even coming in from outside, which means all the street lights are out, too. It's a real blizzard, and we're right in the middle of it.

♦ ♦ ♦

Being as careful as I can, I put Peg down and make my way over to the cabinets. After quite a bit of rustling around, I'm able to find the flashlight Mom keeps for emergencies. This is definitely an emergency.

I flip it on, and shine it at my sisters. Peggy is sitting on the floor, her dolls forgotten. Lauren is staring at the blank TV screen. They both look frightened. I know my own face probably looks the same, so I offer them a comforting smile.

I go over to the phone to call Mrs. Duncan. I want to ask her if her electricity is out, too—but the phone isn't working either.

"I'm cold," says Lauren.

"You are?" Then, I notice the chill. I go over to our space heater and gently tap it. I tap it again and feel it with my hand. The space heater is still warm, but it isn't releasing any more heat. Without thinking I say, "The heater went out."

"It did?" Lauren cries. "How will we keep warm?"

Before Peggy can join in with her own tears, I say, "We'll make a tent and huddle together tonight while we sleep."

"We will?" Peggy says excitedly. "Can I help?"

"Sure thing. It'll be fun."

We fumble our way through the house with the flashlight. We take the quilts, sheets, and blankets off all the beds—ours and Mom's. For good measure, I grab a bunch of pillows.

"Lauren? Peggy?" I say, as we creep back to the living room.

"Yeah?" My sisters are right behind me.

"You stay here. I'm going to go into the kitchen to get some chairs," I tell them.

Lauren shoots me a scared look. "You're going to leave us here? Alone? With the monsters?"

Peggy's eyes grow wide. "Monsters?"

Lauren nods. "I saw a special about snow monsters on TV."

"Lauren," I say in exasperation, not even wanting to know how she found time to watch that between all her game shows. "You don't really believe in snow monsters, do you?"

Lauren shrugs. "They had pictures and everything."

Tears stream down Peggy's cheeks. "Don't let the monsters eat me!"

"See what you started?" I say to Lauren. I kneel down to Peggy's level. "Peg, there are *no* monsters in Vermont. Besides, not all monsters are bad. Look at Cookie Monster."

Peggy's eyes clear. "Cookie Monster wouldn't eat me."

The flashlight is starting to flicker. I have to get this tent built. I rush into the kitchen for the chairs. I drag them to the living room one by one, arrange them strategically around the room, and throw the heaviest quilts, blankets, and some pillows into the center. Then, I carefully drape some sheets and lightweight blankets over the chairs to fashion our tent.

We just stand there for a little bit and admire our creation. Snow continues to drum down on the roof. I never knew snow could make so much noise.

"Haley, I'm tired," Peggy announces.

I check my watch. It's still a couple hours before Peggy usually goes to sleep, but the house is getting colder. "Bedtime!"

Neither of my sisters complains. We crawl into our tent, pile the covers up on top of us, and snuggle in together. It's actually kinda comfy.

"Haley," says Peggy as I fluff up her pillow, "Mom will be here when I wake up, right?"

"Don't worry. She'll be home before we know it."

Peggy smiles and closes her eyes. I lean over to Lauren.

"What if we freeze to death?" Lauren whispers to me.

"We won't freeze. We'll keep each other warm, and you're under a lot of blankets."

Lauren thinks about that for a moment. "I'm scared."

"We'll be fine," I say, mostly believing it. "Just go to sleep. The power will be on when we wake up. Mom will come home, and she'll make us breakfast."

I listen to the wind howl outside. Again, I think of Jake. I'm mad at him now. My sisters need me! He and I can go see that stupid movie anytime. But I also can't help remembering that, when Jake and I *do* see each other, he usually is pretty cool.

I don't know how much later it is when I finally fall asleep.

◆ ◆ ◆

I wake up to a loud noise. I reach for my alarm, but it isn't where it's supposed to be. I open one eye, and everything comes flooding back to me. The snowstorm, Mom stuck at work, sleeping on the floor. Then, I realize the ringing I hear is the phone. I make my way out of the tent and run for it. "Hello?"

"Haley, how is everything?" It's Mom. "Are you girls okay? The power and phones went out here at the office. I've been trying to call you all night from my cell phone but couldn't get through. Did the phones go out at home, too?"

"There's been no power, but we had a campout in the living room. Lauren and Peggy are still sleeping."

"I knew you could handle things." Mom lets out a huge sigh of relief. "They finally reopened the roads, and the plows are going through. I'm going to head home right now."

"Can you bring us something for breakfast?" I ask.

"Anything you want!" she says.

"Mom, whatever is fine. Just come home." I hang up and breathe my own sigh of relief. As if on cue, the power comes back on.

"Haley?" Peggy calls from the tent. "Where's Mommy?"

"She just called. She'll be here soon."

Lauren wakes up, too, and notices the power on before she notices Mom still isn't home. "Finally!" she shouts as she crawls out of the tent and makes a mad dash for the TV in the kitchen. Peggy comes out behind her.

I sit quietly while Peggy plays with her dolls.

Then, there's a knock at the door.

"Who's there?" I call, assuming Mrs. Duncan has finally gotten Mom's messages and is coming over to check on us.

"Haley? It's Jake."

JAKE. "Jake? What are you doing here?" I call, as I stand up to unlock the door.

Once I reach it, in walks a sheepish-looking Jake, followed by...Mom!

"Mommy!" shouts Peggy, running toward her. Lauren races toward her too and we all embrace in a long group hug.

"Girls, how are you? Is everyone all right?"

"Haley took care of us," says Lauren.

"Yeah," agrees Peggy, "She didn't let the monsters eat us."

"Monsters?" Mom repeats, shooting me a questioning look.

"We survived," I tell Mom.

"Mommy?" Peggy asks, hanging onto Mom's arms as she takes off her coat. "I'm hungry."

Mom gives Peggy a kiss. "I brought home some frozen waffles for breakfast and a special surprise for dessert."

They all go into the kitchen. I stay where I am and turn to Jake. "How did you get here?"

"My dad drove me in his truck. He'll come back in about an hour to get me. I just wanted to make sure you were all okay, and I thought you might need your driveway shoveled or something."

"Maybe we can do it together after we eat." I am so happy to see him. "Did you go to the movie?"

"In this weather? *No way!* Maybe we can go this weekend."

"Sounds good to me. Come on. Let's go get waffles before they're all gone."

We go into the kitchen and sit down at the table. Frozen waffles never tasted so good, and the whole bunch is gone in a few minutes. Even Peggy, usually a picky eater, has two.

"Guess what I have for dessert?" Mom says. "Chocolate cake!"

Lauren and Peggy (especially Peggy) cheer. Mom, Jake, and I just smile.

◆ ◆ ◆

Old Friends

Kimberly Feltes

Summer has ended, Sadie Blake has returned to school, and she's just made the biggest decision of her life. Will she make it through the year?

I woke up. No, that's not true. I merely opened my eyes. I hadn't even been asleep. Truth is, I hadn't slept all night. Something terrible had happened. And I knew that the rest of my life was going to be miserable. Absolutely miserable. And there was nothing I could do about it.

"Mom!" I yelled out. No response. "Mom!" I cried again.

That one got her. I think it was the little squeal I threw in at the end. She came running into my room. "What, Sadie? What is it?" she asked.

But I couldn't tell her. It was just too awful. I flopped back into my bed and pulled the covers over my face. Then, I realized this was it, my moment of truth. I had to come clean. Keeping quiet was killing me.

"I'm the one who threw the rock," I whispered.

"*What?*" she said.

But I knew she had heard me. And I knew she knew exactly what I was talking about. I'm sure the *whole town* knew what I was talking about.

The day before, someone had broken a window at Brian Dull's house. I'm not joking. That really *is* his last name. And it's a perfect fit. But it wasn't always his last name. His mom just remarried, and Brian took his new step-dad's name. Not sure I would have gone that route, no matter how much I liked the guy. But that's beside the point.

What really matters is that I broke his window. That's right. It was me. And how did I do it? Yep. By throwing a rock. Now, here's the hard part. Why? Why did I do it?

That's what my mom kept asking me, anyway.

The answer isn't so easy. Especially because it doesn't have much to do with Brian. Well, maybe a little. But, really, it has to do with Jody Martin, my former best friend.

It all started about a week ago, just as summer was ending. Well, truth is, it started years ago. But I'll get to that later. For now, you only need to know the recent events.

Jody lives two blocks away from me, and we're best friends. Correction, we *were* best friends.

We were quite a pair. I envied her long blonde hair, thin frame, and the fact that she was always so sure of herself. I wished I could be more like that. I used to tell her so all the time.

She would say, "You're too nice. You've gotta be tougher." She would never admit this, but I think she wanted to be more like me— even in height. She had no idea, though, what a pain it was to be so tall. Especially now that I had outgrown most of the boys in our class. We used to joke that all our opposite traits added up to one complete person.

But things changed just before school started. I'm not sure why. Maybe *I'm* the one who changed. Maybe I just couldn't deal with her anymore.

Here's what I mean: About a week before school started, Jody and I were at the pool at the community center. No one else was around. But then Jason, the cutest boy in our class, showed up.

I had such a crush on him, it almost hurt. He was gorgeous. He had blond hair and beautiful green eyes. And best of all, he was really tall. He had at least two inches on me. In school, I always blushed when I looked in his direction. I couldn't even imagine actually talking to him.

But here at the pool, things seemed different. I felt relaxed, despite the fact that I was wearing a bikini for the first time in my life. It just seemed so easy to talk to him. That was probably because no one was around. Jason was really popular. And, well, I wasn't.

Don't get me wrong. I wasn't *unpopular*. I just wasn't one of the "cool" kids. But Jason definitely was. Anyway, he and I ended up swimming in the pool together. We raced each other a couple of times, then sat on the steps and hung out a bit. When Jason had to leave, he lightly tugged on one of my braids as he got out of the pool.

"See you around," he said. The way he smiled at me made me think he just might like me.

Once Jason was gone, Jody got into the pool. I had asked her to join Jason and me several times, but she had just rolled her eyes and gone back to reading her magazine.

"You know, he doesn't like you," she said. "He just wanted to get a good look at you in your bikini."

I felt *really* embarrassed. I don't know why. Maybe I was worried that Jody was right. I mean, why would Jason be interested in me? All the popular girls were perfect-looking. They had silky skin and long, glossy hair. And in case I haven't mentioned it yet, that's not what I look like.

I have freckles and ratty reddish-brown hair. My mom says it's wavy. But she always says nice things about me. All I know is that my hair frizzes out at the mere mention of rain, so that's why I mostly wear it in braids. Of course, then I look like a seven-year-old—a really *tall* seven-year-old. But that's better than looking like a crazy person.

I told Jody I needed to get home to do some chores. Truth was, I just didn't feel like being around her anymore. Why did she have to make me feel so bad about myself?

But it was more than that. I was scared. Jody had never turned on me before, but sometimes Jody could get ugly. Like the time in school last year when she made Sarah Heath cry just for wearing a turtleneck. I mean, who cares? I guess Jody did.

It was lunch break, and Sarah was sitting a few seats down from us, eating alone. Her thin brown hair was pulled back in a tiny brown barrette. And she wore a solid red turtleneck that looked too big on her rail-thin frame.

Suddenly, Jody turned to her. "Don't you know you look like a dork wearing that plain turtleneck?" Then Jody looked at Kari, who was sitting across from us. "Don't turtlenecks look dumb without a sweater over them?" Kari just nodded.

I cringed a bit—but was relieved I hadn't worn a turtleneck that day. A lot of kids were afraid of Jody, but no one ever stood up to her. *Ever.*

Not even when she razzed pudgy Laura for eating ice cream sandwiches every day. And not when she teased Darrin over and over for talking about *Cuban* artists in class when he meant to say *cubist* artists. But now, her bullying was really starting to bother me. Probably because, this time, *I* was her target.

It happened again a few days later at the tennis courts when Amy Sanders asked if she could play with Jody and me for a while. She didn't have a racket, and I offered her mine so she could hit with Jody. But Jody insisted Amy take her racket and play with me. So, that's what we did.

Amy's a great player and gave me more of a run than Jody ever had. I didn't win a single point but had a blast anyway. We played for a while, and then I offered to trade off with Jody. She said no. So, Amy and I played a bit longer. I was really sweating, but still hadn't won a point. Finally, Amy had to go.

"You know, she just wanted to play with a loser so she could win," Jody hissed at me as Amy walked off. It was such a dumb thing to say. But I didn't care. I figured Jody was probably just annoyed at having to sit there for so long. I tried again to get her to play with me. But she stormed off.

Then, I saw Jason walking toward the tennis courts. I wasn't sure what to do. He came closer. "Hey, you!" he called out.

I waved and kind of smiled. But I made it clear I was heading out. Jody had put me in a really foul mood. And, I didn't want to seem cranky around Jason. Not that it mattered. I'm sure he was just being nice. There was no way he *really* liked me.

I started thinking about things. Mostly, I wondered why Jody was being so mean to me. I wondered if things would get worse or go back to normal. Then I thought about what "normal" meant. I guess it meant Jody picking on other people, but not me.

Suddenly, I felt really bad for never having stuck up for anyone. And why didn't I? Well, Jody was fun. She was up for anything. She would think of things to do that never would have crossed my mind. Like the time we used her blow-up water raft to slide down a huge hill after a two-day snowstorm. Or when we snuck down to the creek after dark one night to look for ghosts.

But remember when I said this all started years ago? Well, I didn't always live in this town. A few years back, I was the new kid in town. I was shy—and *filled* with terror. I obsessed about how no one would like me. How no one would eat with me. How no one would pick me for their team in gym class. On and on, I dreamt up all kinds of awful scenarios in which I was always the loser.

But then I ran into Jody one day while walking to the library. She invited me over to her house. So I went. And that's when it happened. This thing that's kept me quiet all these years.

I remember feeling really happy that I had made a friend. We baked cookies, ate candy, drank Kool-Aid, jumped on her bed, and laughed. Everything was great. Then, I started to feel kind of sick. I got up and walked down the hall to the bathroom. I felt worse with every step. *How long was this hallway?* I wondered. I thought I would never make it to the bathroom.

But I did. And then, I threw up. Problem was, none of it went into the toilet. It seemed to have gone everywhere else.

I couldn't believe it. I squeezed my eyes shut, clenched my fists, and imagined that I had only eaten four cookies, not seven. I'm sure you'll be surprised to hear it, but when I opened my eyes, the mess was *still* there.

Jody came to see if I was all right, but I felt humiliated. I barely knew this girl and it wasn't a pretty sight. *Trust me.*

But Jody was really cool about the whole thing. She called in her mom, who cleaned everything up. Jody and I stood there while her mom kept muttering about how she had just bought the bathmat. I thought I was going to cry.

But then Jody started making funny faces at me. When she crossed her eyes and stuck her tongue out like a dog, I couldn't help but giggle a bit. Jody's mom shot me a look that still haunts me today.

The next day, I met Jody at the bus stop. It was my first day at my new school. Behind her, a short, thick-legged kid ran toward us. Jody looked back. "Here comes the dork," she said. I worried for a second that she would tell everyone what I had done. Then she gave me a little smile, and I figured that meant I was in. And I was right. We became best friends. I found out later that the "dork" was a kid named Brian.

I have no idea why she didn't tear me apart back then. Think about it. She had the power to ruin my life. But she didn't tease me at all. And she didn't say a word to anyone. Maybe for once in her life she felt sorry for someone.

I didn't think about it too much back then. All I knew was that I was happy she was keeping my secret. I thought she was the greatest friend. And for a long time, I refused to see her as someone who could be mean.

But, all of that changed yesterday. It was Friday, the second day back to school. Jody, Brian, a few others, and I were waiting for the bus. Jody started in on Brian. I had hoped things would be different this year, but apparently they weren't.

She went right up to him. "Why'd you change your last name, huh?" she pestered him. "He's not even your dad. Why'd you take his last name? Especially a name like Dull."

No one did anything to stop her. Not even me. I just looked at the grass. But I sensed Brian's face reddening as he turned away from Jody. She kept circling him and pounding him with questions.

When the bus came, Brian hurriedly sank into a seat behind the driver. The other kids disappeared into the middle seats. Jody and I went to the back. I turned to the window and watched the trees go by.

More and more kids got on the bus. Something in me boiled over. I looked at Jody. "I don't like what you just did," I said.

"What are you talking about?" she responded.

"At the bus stop."

She didn't say anything.

"It was mean," I continued.

"Are you for real?" she yelled at me.

"I think it was mean," I said again.

"I just wanted to know what the deal is with his name," she said.

I didn't say anything for a moment. Then, quietly, I said the words that changed everything for me. "I don't think I can be your friend anymore."

She looked at me…then moved to the seat across the aisle. "You know," she said, "you've been a real brat all summer, Sadie Blake. I've been waiting for you to turn on me. So, fine. We're not friends anymore."

We didn't talk the rest of the way to school. I was really scared. I don't remember going into the building. I don't even remember my classes. I just remember thinking people were whispering about me all day. I swear some kids pointed at me. And I think Jimmy Kane even made throw-up noises as I passed him in the hall.

I was mortified. And I was angry. At myself. And at Brian Dull. I just wanted to take it back. All of it.

Instead, after school, I threw a rock at Brian's basement window. I don't know why, but I was shocked when I heard the glass break. I really thought the rock would just bounce off the window.

When the glass shattered, I turned and ran. All the way home. I slipped into bed and stayed there. All night. All morning. Until I just couldn't bear it anymore. So, I told my mom everything. And then I cried. She held me tightly and said it would be okay.

"No, it won't," I sobbed, "I know Jody told. They're all going to make fun of me now."

"No one will even remember on Monday," she said. But I didn't believe her. And there was one thing I knew for sure. Jason would never like me now. I mean, who likes a girl who pukes at people's houses?

My mom hugged me again and then went to make me breakfast. Usually, I make it myself, but I think she wanted to do something nice for me. I got out of bed and went over to my computer. I turned it on and checked my e-mail. I wanted to see if I had any friends left.

There was just one message. It was from a *JTM928*. *Who the heck was that?* I opened it up, dreading the worst. Then, I smiled. The message read: *"Hey there! Remind me to tell you about the time I puked in gym class after running hurdles. And I'm not talking about when I was in kindergarten."*

It was signed, *"Jason."*

Maybe my life wouldn't be so miserable after all.

Just Perfect

Kristi Collier Thompson

If you want to succeed, you have to find…perfection.

There are certain rules you have to follow if you want to succeed in middle school. You have to know what to wear, what to say, what classes to take, even, apparently, what boys to hang out with.

The rules aren't written down or even talked about much. They are passed down from generation to generation, from mother to daughter to little sister. It's a kind of ritual—something that takes place during those mother-daughter back-to-school shopping sprees. All of which would have been well and good, except that I didn't have a mother. And I didn't know the rules.

I couldn't ask my dad for help. He was wonderful and understanding, but he was quite obviously a man. He was also, even by the loosest standards, *weird*. It was a zany, lovable kind of weird, but let's face it—in middle school, weird is weird. He is a zoological specialist, and he has a tendency to break into spontaneous discussion about elephant dung. No, I couldn't ask him.

Fortunately, my best friends, Rachel and Natalie, took the matter into their capable, well-manicured, and we-both-have-hip-moms-who-were-once-high-school-homecoming-queens hands.

"That's the one, Kia," Natalie said as I emerged from the dressing room in her favorite store. "It's perfect!"

Rachel studied me critically and nodded. "It is. It's perfect," she echoed.

I stared at myself in the dressing room mirror and pursed my lips. "You really think so?" I liked the first outfit I had tried on better. It was more colorful and fun. This one was all pinks and creams and skin. *My* skin. I shivered. I guess I looked okay, but the outfit just seemed so...

"Perfect!" Natalie repeated. "See, you're doing great. Sharp, put-together, always in control." She smoothed my hair so that it lay flat against my back.

I shrugged. "If you say so."

By the time we finished shopping, I had five perfect outfits, with matching shoes and a new purse. I was famished. A headache was beginning to form behind my right eye. I wondered if my mom had liked shopping. When I asked Dad, he laughed and said her favorite outfit had been a pair of paint-stained jeans with patches that matched the colors on the walls in our house. I had those jeans tucked away in a drawer in my dresser. They always made me smile.

Rachel, Natalie and I weaseled my dad into buying a pizza and then driving us back to my house. We holed up in my room with our food, our diet sodas, and our new class schedules. Two more days until school started. I didn't think I would ever be ready.

"We all have lunch together. That's good," Natalie declared for what must have been the tenth time. "Buy it, don't bag it." She looked my way.

I stopped with a piece of pizza halfway to my mouth. "Okay, okay," I said. I was infamous at Harris Elementary School for packing whatever leftovers we had in the house and eating them cold the next day for lunch. I also make a killer meatball sub. But if cafeteria food was part of the middle school deal, then so be it.

"You really have a good schedule, Kia," Rachel said. "Oh, and guess what?" She leaned in excitedly. "I heard from Aaron Walters that he and Jacob Sanders both have English third period! Isn't that great? We'll have to find a way to sit close to them." Rachel winked conspiratorially. I felt my stomach sink and wondered why. Jacob Sanders had been one of the cutest boys at Harris Elementary School. He'd be just as cute at Rosemount Middle School, I was sure. Rachel had been trying to get us together for months. It was just that Jacob was so...

"Perfect!" Natalie said. "He's perfect, Kia. Really."

"See, aren't you glad I talked you out of that pottery elective?" Rachel said. "Now you can take English with me *and* Jacob." She sang his name. "Pottery would have messed everything up."

"Yeah, I guess so." I had really wanted to take pottery, but...

I leaned against my bed and sighed. I was glad Rachel and Natalie were helping me. I just wished the rules were a little less...

a little less...rule-like. I wasn't sure how good I was going to be at being perfect.

◆ ◆ ◆

I woke up early on Monday morning. The air was balmy, but a slight breeze ruffled my curtains. Rachel and Natalie said they were little girl curtains, but I couldn't bear to part with them. My mom had redecorated my room, curtains included, for my seventh birthday, just weeks before she died.

I sighed and took her picture off the nightstand, so I could hold it close. I traced the outline of her face. Dad always said I look like her, but I couldn't see it. I was gawky and plain and always tripping over my own feet. She had been beautiful and talented and... perfect! I sat up quickly, which caused my room to spin slightly.

"So what do *you* think?" I asked her picture. "About the clothes and the classes and the boys? What would you do?"

She stared back at me, smiling and unblinking. I frowned and placed the picture back on the nightstand.

"That's what I was afraid of," I said. I walked to my closet. I guessed my mother hadn't been perfect after all. She had died of a brain tumor, an abnormality. It was imperfection that had killed her.

I got dressed in my new outfit and walked into the kitchen. Dad was sitting at the table, eating a leftover egg-salad sandwich. "Want some?" he asked absentmindedly, waving his fork. He was deep into an article about parasitic worms.

"No, thanks," I said. "I'll just have some coffee. Black."

"Okay," Dad mumbled. Then he stopped, marked his place with his finger, and swiveled his head toward me. "Hey, you don't drink coffee...Hey!" He raised his eyebrows. "You look....Wow. You look different." He stood up and walked around me.

I followed him with my eyes. "Different good or different bad?" I asked.

He cocked his head. "Good, I guess. But you don't look like you." He wrinkled his forehead. "But you're growing up, I guess. First day of middle school." He snapped his fingers. "Oh. That reminds me. Wait right here."

I waited while Dad ran into the other room. I could hear him rummaging through the storage closet. I poured myself a glass of orange juice and buttered a piece of toast. He returned after a few minutes with a bulky package wrapped in brown paper.

"What is it?" I asked as he handed it to me.

"Open it," he said.

I tore off the paper, and then opened the box. A figure, carved out of soapstone, nestled among the tissue paper. I pulled it out and placed it on the table. It was a girl, her arms stretched high, her head thrown back, her face lit by a radiant smile.

"This is one of Mom's, isn't it?" I asked in a whisper. I traced the cool, clean lines of the figurine.

Dad nodded. "She made it for you, just before...just before..." his voice cracked. "She wanted you to have something special at a special time!"

I swallowed a lump that had formed in my throat. My mom had been a sculptor, a good one, too. We had a few of her pieces, but she had sold most of them at fairs and art shows. "It's beautiful," I said, and it was. The stone was smooth and the expression on the girl's face was one of pure joy.

"I told her you would love it. She was worried because...well, it's not one of her best."

I nodded. That's how they first discovered that Mom was sick. Her work had started to suffer. She got dizzy and her hands shook, and she couldn't make the carvings look the way she imagined in her mind.

"It's perfect," I whispered. It wasn't, not really. One of the girl's legs was longer than the other, and her hair had etch marks

where it shouldn't, and the fingers weren't right, but her face...
the look of joy on her face.

"I'll be right back." I ran up to my room and put the figurine
next to my mother's picture. "Thanks, Mom," I said. Then, I finished
getting ready for school. I ran back downstairs just as the doorbell
rang. Rachel and Natalie. We were going to carpool to school. No
buses. I guess that was another rule.

"Different outfit?" Dad asked as he walked toward the front door.

I nodded.

"Whew. For a minute there, I thought I was losing my parental
powers of observation." He opened the front door. "Well, well.
Natalie and Rachel. What a surprise!"

"Good morning, Dr. Achison," Natalie said to my dad. "Ready,
Kia? We want to get there early so we can check out the scene by
our lockers."

I nodded and slung my backpack over my shoulder. I wanted
to get there early, too, but for another reason. I wanted to talk to
my guidance counselor about another change in my schedule.

"Um, Kia?" Rachel studied me, a slight frown on her face.
"What are you wearing?"

I exchanged a quick glance with my dad. He winked. I grinned.
"They're jeans," I said simply. "They were my mother's."

"Yes, but why are you wearing them to school?" Rachel was
still fixated on my outfit. "They're so..."

"*Perfect*," I said. "They are just *perfect*."

♦ ♦ ♦

Author Info

Kristi Collier Thompson (Popularity Rules, Just Perfect) *wrote the novels* Jericho Walls, *winner of the Josette Frank Award for Fiction, and* The Girls' Guide to Dreams.

Emilie Ostrander (Being the Bigger Person, Morning Girls) *lives in Chicago, Illinois, and is a freelance journalist for the* Chicago Tribune. *As a kid, she had a very long walk to school and prefers taking trains everywhere.*

Carolyn Mackler (The Dog Formerly Known as Victor Maximilian Bonaparte Lincoln Rothbaum, Confessions of a Movie Star Extra) *is the author of the book* Love and Other Four-Letter Words. *Her latest teen novel is* The Earth, My Butt, and Other Big Round Things. *She contributes often to* GL.

Wendy Mass (The Invisible Boy) *is the author of a teen novel,* A Mango-Shaped Space, *and the upcoming* Leap Day.

Laura Perdie Salas (How to Catch a Dog Food Snatcher) *grew up in Florida and couldn't wait to escape the heat. She now enjoys all four seasons (yep, even winter) in Minnesota with her husband and two daughters, Maddy and Annabelle. She's written many nonfiction books, and her short stories have been published in magazines such as* Turtle, New Moon, Guideposts for Kids, *and more.*

Patricia Bridgman (Graduation) *is a journalist by training and now writes about amusing kids, (mostly) kind and well-meaning adults, and talented dogs. Her stories appear in the following magazines:* Highlights, Cricket, AIM, Story Friends, Calliope, *as well as on* weeonesmag.com.

Alison Embrey (Sergeant Beckles) *is a fiction, poetry, and magazine writer who lives in Atlanta, Georgia. Growing up a "military brat," Alison went to several different schools as a child because of her father's job working for the U.S. government. In her spare time, Alison reads books by great authors, writes stories on her computer, and watches way too much reality TV.*

Kristen Weber (The Blizzard) *graduated from Binghamton University, where she majored in English. She works in book publishing and lives in Manhattan.*

Kimberly Feltes (Old Friends) *is a writer living in New York City. She was inspired to write "Old Friends," her first short story, after attending her high school reunion. Like Sadie, she once had to make a tough choice about friendship. She's also written an advice book for teens,* Yo Yolanda! Advice From An Expert.

♦ *And, an extra-special thanks to our two youngest GL authors,*
Mary Grace Joseph (The Anonymous Birthday Club) *and*
Diana Koulechova (The Crush Crisis).